MY BESTIES 2

THE TAKE OVER

NOVEL

ASIA HILL

GOOD 2 GO PUBLISHING

ISBN: 978-1-943686-73-5
Copyright ©2015
Published 2015 by Good2Go Publishing
7311 W. Glass Lane • Laveen, AZ 85339
www.good2gopublishing.com
twitter @good2gobooks
G2G@good2gopublishing.com
Facebook.com/good2gopublishing
ThirdLane Marketing: Brian James
Brian@good2gopublishing.com
Cover design: Davida Baldwin
Interior Layout: Mychea, Inc

Printed in the U.S.A.

Acknowledgements

All praises are due to Allah. I feel so blessed and highly favored.

My lovely 3-J's, Jae'lyn, Ja'taya, and Jacob. I'll always try my best to give you the best. I love you more than words can ever express.

To my niece Mikayla and my nephews Meki and Anthony, I can't wait to spoil you guys rotten. To my brother Roger and my sisters Shante' and Roy'el, I love y'all too death. I don't like the distance between us. We need to get that in order because we are all we got.

To my entire family. Look, thanks to Joseph Melvin Campbell, Jr. and Elizabeth Louise Yates-Campbell, I don't have enough paper space to shout out everybody. So, let's do this. If you are related to me, know that I love y'all.

I want to personally thank all of my haters. Twitter got the followers and I got y'all. Thank you for all the lies you told about me, all the negative things that you said, and I want to thank the ones that smiled in my face and rolled their eyes behind my back. I wanted to get back at you in the best way that I knew how. My success is my best revenge. I'll never stop succeeding...Get on my level!

To my fallen stars. Lamont "Bingo" Williams, Antoine "Mookie" Singleton, Tyshawn Walker, Edricko "Woodie" Perkins, and J. R. Steele. There's not a day that goes by that you're not missed. Rest in Paradise. I dedicate this book to you.

A special shout out to my besties. I'm mad at y'all, but I still love y'all. Katari, Bessie, Mona, Kita, and Kia. We ran them streets over East with our stomp-a-chick game. I miss y'all so much! Cora Hopkins and Shaun Rushing you know how much I love you girls! Brandi "Chuck" Johnson, where the book at man? If I missed you, it wasn't personal. Charge it to my mind, not my heart.

To my special bestie Miranda, I told you that this was gonna be a bumpy ride. I'm still riding! Thank you for pushing me to get this book out. Who loves you? They can say what they want. They just mad… You know I love you girl!

Lindell, you are amazing! Every day you show me just how wonderful it is to know you. I appreciate the effort and I love you because you the shit, baby! Heidi, I didn't forget about you, ole crazy ass lady. Hugs and kisses to you.

Good2Go, we got another hit! Let's get it!

MY BESTIES 2

THE TAKE OVER

1 ~ Lil Mama

"Hi, you've reached Boo. Leave a message."
"Bitch! How you gon tell me to come get you and now you not answering the phone!" I hung up the phone, mad as fuck; I hate that shit! I've got so many thoughts running through my head right now. I know that she's going to tell me that she's back in the game. "UGGH!" I'm frustrated.

When she was on, it was love. We didn't have to worry about money, but fuck...I'm on parole! Federal parole at that.

"What the fuck?" I pull up on the block and police and ambulances are everywhere. While looking for a parking spot I hear my name being called. "LIL MAMA, GET OUT! GET OUT!" I see my niece's friend running up to my car.

"What the hell is going on?" She's breathing so hard that I can barely understand her. "Calm down! Now tell me what's wrong."

"SOMEBODY SHOT BOO!" That's all I hear come out of her mouth before I push her little ass out of my way and take off running at full speed up the block. I make it to her yard before a police officer grabs me.

ASIA HILL

"Ma'am, you can't go in there."

"LET ME GO! THAT'S MY SISTER'S HOUSE!"

He wasn't letting up, which sends me through the roof. "LET ME THE FUCK GO! WHERES MY SISTER?" I'm screaming at the top of my lungs when the paramedics bring my sister out on a stretcher.

"BOO?! BOO?! WHO DID THIS?! WAKE UP, PLEASEEEEE!"

My pleas went fell deaf ears because she wasn't responding. "LET ME GO, PLEASE! SHE FUCKING NEEDS ME!"

I'm now jumping up and down, acting a fucking fool because this pussy-ass police officer won't let me go. "Ma'am, I'mma cuff you if you don't calm down."

I let them load her up into the ambulance. "Ah Woodie, get my car and follow the ambulance!" I readied myself to jump into the ambulance when the paramedic grabbed me. "LET ME GO! I'M RIDING WITH MY SISTER!"

The paramedic looked down and then back up at me. "Ma'am, she's nonresponsive." I'm having a hard time understanding what he's saying. "She needs me! Please let me ride with her!" The last thing I heard before I saw black was, "I'm sorry, but she's gonna be DOA."

LJ

Man, shit been crazy this whole summer. Within two months, I met a chick, fell in love with her, accidently helped her and her besties rob a bank, and then witnessed several murders.

The little chick and her besties came up in a major way. I haven't seen a chick who's more about that life, but man Joe, with the good came the bad. My best friend is in the hospital fighting for his life. We got this crazy ass nigga, Big Moe on the prowl. Both of his cousins are dead because of somebody in our crew.

I need my homie to get right; we got this money to make. We also need to find Big Moe and send his ass on a one-way ticket to hell. My Auntie Boo blessed us with her Jamaican connect. Now that's a boss bitch, for real! Man, I swear that lady is untouchable. With her back in the game, I'm sure we're about to hit that millionaire status sooner rather than later.

I'm really trying to make enough dough so that my boo, Ju, can relax and finish school. I don't want her out here in these streets doing all this crazy shit.

I've got a feeling that her little ass will turn out to be a part of this bullshit. It doesn't help when her three best friends are all about this life. I have never seen three young chicks who go so hard. Sadly, murder is a part of that equation.

When I saw ReRe shoot that lady at the bank, I was stuck. But what took the cake was when my girl popped Boogie's ass without hesitation. I've been in the streets for only a minute and I have never laid a nigga down. I never had to. I know for a fact that I'mma pop Big Moe's ass though.

"Excuse me Sir, your friend wants to see you."

"Thank you." I walk back to Poohman's room, happy to see my boy sitting up on his own. That bullet to his stomach fucked him up. It hit a few of his organs and now it's lodged in his back, only a few inches from his spinal cord.

"What it do?"

"Bro, she gone," he said crying.

I looked at his ass as if he was on fire. I have never seen Poohman cry. I instantly began crying. "Who's gone?"

I woulda sat down, had I known what he was about to say. Maybe I wouldn't have hurt myself, because what he said next brought me to my knees…hard!

"Auntie Boo! He shot her! SHE'S GONE, JAW!"

JuJu

Hey y'all! Back in the mafucka for round two. I hope y'all enjoyed our come up. We did that! Don't sleep on the Eastside of Chicago. We them boys… Well, in our case, we them girls. This was by far the best and worse summer of my life. I met my boo, LJ, and that was probably the best part! We hit a lick for $350,000. I mean, really! I didn't think I had the nerve.

I'm a fighter. I love to fight, but fighting and killing are two different things. I never thought in a million years that I would kill somebody, but when my besties safety are at stake, I'm laying that ass down! I sounded so tough saying that, didn't I?

Let me stop stunting. I was scared as shit when I shot that boy. I don't even think I actually pulled the trigger. The nerve in my finger did, but hey, we got out of there. We got away with $808,517. I'm hooked!

Kids our age ain't never seen that much money. I feel like we're able to hit a few more banks, get our high school diplomas, and move the fuck around. I'm tired of Chicago. All we know is struggle. Ain't shit handed to us. The only thing that's guaranteed is a trip to the morgue. Don't get caught slipping; it's hard out here.

I got things to do. I need to make sure my cousin Tyesha is taken care of since my Auntie Tae ain't shit. The bitch ain't 'bout nothing. She has always hated me. Why? I used to wonder why, but now fuck her.

I need to really have a talk with my Auntie Lil Mama. I know she found that money in my closet. When I went to get a few dollars, I could tell that it had been moved. I'm scared to know what she's thinking. That lady is crazy is hell! Jail really changed her, though she's still my favorite auntie, but she's strict and hella paranoid. I guess eight years in federal prison will do that to you. I know that her ass almost had a stroke when she found that money.

The worst part of all this is watching my bestie's man, Poohman, fight for his life. She's going through it, and I'm just there for support. My boo needs me too. I got strength in me that I never knew I had, like now. I've been running around all day gathering clothes for Jaw, as well as food and personals for ReRe, E, and Tiki. We turned Poohman's room into a studio apartment, and threw the nurses a few dollars so they would leave us be.

I'm sitting at the light on 83rd when Yates and I see an ambulance coming up behind me at full speed. "Damn! Let me move over before I need an ambulance for my damn self!"

As I veered to the right, I saw my auntie's car flying behind it. I look in the car as it passed and I see that she's not in it. Instead, I see my friend Woodie flying down the street driving her car.

"Uh...Un! What the fuck?" I hit my auntie's phone. No answer. "I know this mafucka ain't stole my auntie's shit and round her joy riding! I'mma fuck him up!"

I smashed down on the gas pedal. My lil Cutless got some power under the hood, because about three seconds later, I was on his ass.

BEEP! BEEEEEEP!

"ROLL DOWN THE WINDOW!"

He was mouthing something that I couldn't understand and pointing at the ambulance at the same time.

"WHAT?"

He finally rolled the window down. "FOLLOW ME!"

"WHERE IS MY AUNTIE?"

"SHE'S IN THE AMBULANCE!"

"WHAT?" Oh my stars! Why is she in the ambulance?

We turned left on 79th and headed towards the Dan Ryan Expressway. Ten minutes later, we pulled up to the same hospital as Poohman. I jumped outta the car, barely putting it in park.

I rushed towards the ambulance that Woodie said my aunt was in. I saw that Woodie was on my heels. "Ju wait! Come here! Wait!"

"No, what's wrong with my auntie?"

He grabbed my arm. "LET ME GO, WOODIE! I NEED TO FIND OUT ---" he says, while shaking the shit outta me.

"Calm down! She's fine! She blacked out!"

"Blacked out? Why?"

He put his head down.

"Why did she black out, Woodie?"

He's still not saying shit, which is pissing me off and scaring me at the same time. Finally, he looks up at me. The tears in his eyes broke me down. I mean, this is my nigga, if he don't get any bigger! I never seen him cry before.

"Man Joe, why you crying? Tell me something, please!"

"Boo's dead."

2 ~ Big Moe

"**I**'m sorry, G-ma. I was supposed to protect them. I let you down. Don't worry, because on everything I love, I'mma make every last one of them pay…in blood!"

I'mma goon ass nigga. I rarely show emotion, but this summer by far was the worst for me. I lost both of my niggas. My cousin Boogie and JR were like brothers. We grew up in the same house. I'm the one who turned them on to getting money. I trusted them, I loved them, and now they are gone. I'm about to go on a murdering rampage. How the fuck did all this shit go down like that?

We were robbed twice by the same people. The nerve of them lil mafuckas. Fucking kids! I'mma kill them and they mama for having them, and they fathers for not flushing they bitch asses.

I got something for that bitch Boo, too! Snake ass hoe! I thought that hoe was official. This is a small world. I really don't think she knew what her peoples were into, but I don't give a fuck. Everybody involved is gonna die.

For now, I'm lying low at my aunt's crib. It kills me to have to look in my cousin's face. She's fourteen, and JR and Boogie were everything to her.

"Ramone, can I live with you for the school year?"

I love how sweet she is. "We'll see. I'mma see if yo big sister gon let us crash over east with her."

My cousin Mia lives on 81st and Burnham. She's low-key over there doing her thang. I need to be in that hood, but in the cut so that I can find them mafuckas who took our shit. JoJo going to school over there, and will keep me in the shadows, but I can find out where them little bitches hang at. I swear, I'mma kill em' slow and painfully.

"JoJo, you hungry?"

"Yeah."

I pulled away from the cemetery and headed towards Leon's Barbeque Rib joint on 79th and Stoney Island. My mind was racing a million miles an hour. The only thing going through my mind was revenge. "JoJo, go in and get me a rib tip and fry dinner. Don't forget ---"

"I know your pineapple wildwood pop."

JoJo

What's up y'all? Things should be simple for me. I'm fourteen and I don't know how I've made it through all the bullshit that I've been through.

My mom died when I was a baby. My G-Ma, my sister Mia, and my brothers raised me. JR and Boogie spoiled me. My sister Mia showed me the girlie things. My cousin Ramone taught me how to fight the lil boys, and my G-Ma taught me how to cook, clean, and iron.

They say death that comes in threes. Well, I lost my G-Ma, Boogie, and JR. Ramone ain't good at the soft sentimental stuff, but he is my rock right now.

I'm about to start my freshman year and I can't wait. I wanna move over east with my sister Mia. It's some cuties in her hood. I need to show these hoes over here what flawless looks like – at 5'3 I weigh 150 pounds.

I inherited my family's hazel eyes. I wear my hair short. I look older than fourteen. You can't tell me shit. But don't let the cuteness fool you. I'm 'bout that life. I fight better than most dudes do.

Growing up in the Cabrini Green projects taught my young ass a few things. I want better for myself. I know getting my education is the key to my future. I just like to have a little fun in the process.

"Let me get two rib tip dinners with fries, no coleslaw, and two pineapple pops."

As I wait for my food, I turn to my left and see this boy I know from my sister's hood. "Hey, Lil Man." He walks towards me with a huge smile on his face. "Sup, JoJo. What you doing over east?"

"Bout to go see if Mia gon let me go to school over here." He smiled even harder. "Aww shit! Come fuck wit cha boy."

I look at the boy walking up on our conversation and I must admit, this nigga was cute as shit. "Lil Man, who is this?"

"Aw my bad. This my homie, Young Meech. He go to my school."

"What up, Young Meech?" He looks me up and down while licking his lips, causing butterflies to swarm in my stomach.

"What's good, Shawty?" Before I can say anything else, here come Ramone's cock blocking ass. "JoJo, I told you to come get some food, not to be a hot ass. Who the fuck is these lil niggas?"

I roll my eyes and made the introductions. "Ramone, this is Lil Man and Young Meech. They live around Mia's house."

He looks at Young Meech. "Ah, lil nigga, you look like my man's that got killed a few years ago."

Young Meech's face turns sour in a matter of seconds. It was almost as if he was mugging Ramone. "The only nigga I look like is my pops." Ramone takes a step back and looks him up and down. "King Meech yo daddy?"

I look back and forth because I can feel the tension building up fast. "He was my daddy. How you know him?"

In a matter of seconds, Ramone's mood changes dramatically. "I used to do business with him. It's a shame what happened to him." He looked at me. "Get the food, and let's go, NOW!"

3 ~ Young Meech

"**M**eech, what the fuck was all that about?" I look at my homie and shake my head. "Man, the way dude said that shit, it sent chills down my spine. I don't know what that was about, but it didn't sit well with me."

We got our food and walked down the 'Nine' eating and fucking with the hoes. I hate when people bring up my pops. I miss that nigga to death. Shit been crazy since he been gone. Before he died, my life was a blessing. Big ass crib overlooking Lake Michigan. I got everything I wanted. I even met a sister that I never knew I had. She was my baby. Tamiko came to stay with us a few years back and it was as if we were meant to be brother and sister.

She looked just like our pops and treated me as if I was her baby. My mom was even nice to her. That was a first because my mother was a bitch. She was always fussing with my daddy about money or bitches. Our lil family was complete until that dreadful first day of August.

It was my sister's birthday and pops told me to get dressed. He was going to take me, Tiki, and her friends to Great America. That was the last time that

I saw him alive. Later on that day, I heard that bell ring. Thinking that it was pops, I ran to the door and opened it. It was the police bringing my sister home. She was shaking all over and she was covered in blood.

"Meech, who's at the door? You know better! Don't be just opening the damn---" My mom stopped dead in her tracks and looked back and forth from the police officer to Miko.

"Where's King? Miko, where's your daddy?"

My sister screamed. "HE...HE...HE...THEY SHOT HIM IN THE HEAD!"

My mom dropped to her knees and screamed. I can still hear the screams that came from the depths of her soul. "UGHHHHH! NO, NOT HIM! PLEASE KING! NOOOOOOO!"

The officer told her to come with them to identify his body. She called her sister to come and watch us. The police escorted her to the hospital. I ran upstairs and started my sister a bath. When I came back downstairs to get her, she was still standing by the door shaking.

"Meechie Pooh, they killed him in front of me."

I told her to come on. "Take a bath and when you finish, we will talk." After she finished her bath, she told me everything that happened, from pops picking her up late from school, the argument he had on the phone, them laughing and rapping that Twista song, to somebody running up to the driver's side window shooting him point blank range in the head.

"What you do after that?"

"I grabbed his hand and called his name." She took a deep breath and began crying. He gripped my hand and told me to grab the backpack in the backseat, take his phone, and give it to you."

I looked at her for a few seconds before I spoke. "To me? What for?"

She shrugged her shoulders. "He said that you'll know what to do. He said he loved us."

She finally broke down. She cried so hard that she made me cry. "He...He...He said it's all her fault."

"Who?"

She wiped her face and looked into my eyes. "Your mother."

That blew the socks off my feet. What the fuck did she have to do with my pops dying? After crying for a few more hours, my sister finally fell asleep. I went downstairs and got the backpack. When I was back in the privacy of my own room, I opened it. "Damn pops," was all I could say. There were stacks of money in rubber bands. Hundreds after hundreds.

I was stuck! What the fuck I'mma do with all this money? I was only nine years old. I dumped all the money on the bed and at the bottom of the bag was an envelope. When I opened it, I cried while reading it. I guess it was my father's last words.

Young Meech,

You and Miko were the reason for my grind. I made some fucked up decisions in my life that ultimately led to my demise. I knew my days were numbered. They didn't call me King for nothing! I put in that work son, so you and Miko could live comfortably. I kept you close so that you would know when it was your turn. I know you young, but you ready! Never let pussy dictate your actions. Trust no bitch, but Miko, when you feel like you ready, call the only number that's saved in my phone. They'll make sure you good.

I put the letter down and began bawling. It was as if he knew, but damn it hurts. This was my pops. My pops was everything to me. As if sensing from the afterlife that I would react like this, the next line in his letter was:

Stop that fucking crying Meech! I'm good! Me and the devil smoking a blunt right now. But for real son, focus. You got everything you need, ok? I love you. One more thing. Don't give your mother, SHIT! You too young to understand, but when you get right

and get your weight up, ask her why Tank? Take care of Miko!

I put the letter back in the bag and put my head down. So many thoughts ran through my head. I dozed off for a few hours. I woulda stayed asleep had I not heard my mother screaming at somebody. "HOW AM I SUPPOSED TO GET THE COMBINATION NOW, DUMBASS? HE'S DEAD!"

I cracked my door so I could hear her clearer. "Why didn't you have the lil bitch shot too? Oh don't worry, you'll get your shit, but I want in that safe first."

After a few seconds of silence, she continued. "I'll meet you at eleven."

I could see Miko walking towards my room, but before she made it, my mother pushed her against the wall. "It's all your fucking fault! If he didn't pick yo ass up from school, he'd still be here!"

I walked in the hallway as if I didn't know what was happening. "Ma, what's wrong? Why you holding her like that?"

"Baby, she's the reason your daddy's dead! He shoulda left her with her whore of a mother! Now he's dead! She can't stay in here another night!"

Before I could say anything, Miko's words cracked my mother's face. "How can you blame me for my daddy's death when you was the one fucking his best friend, Tank?"

I looked at my mother with fire in my eyes. Miko kept talking. "He didn't die right away, just so you know. You been fucking Tank. You was also stealing money from him and giving Tank his work. He told me to tell you that he'll see you in hell! I called Auntie Shawn from Gary, Indiana. She's on the way to get you."

My mother looked as if she was about to pass out. "Sh…Shawn is coming where?" I just looked at my punk ass mama and shook my head. Look at the shit I gotta go through at a young age. My mama ain't shit!

"What you mean, coming to get me? You not coming? Auntie Shawn cool, Miko. Come with us. She look like a boy, but she still cool. Please come!"

"I can't come, Meechie Pooh. I'm going back to my mother's. She needs me."

I started crying.

"Don't cry lil bro."

I wiped my eyes. "But Miko, I want you."

I didn't even know that my mother had dipped off. Miko started walking away. "Where you going?"

She turned back around and gave me a hug. "Go pack your stuff, Tink Tink. It's time to go."

DING DONG!

DING DONG!

I ran downstairs to open the door. "Who is it?"

"Shawn."

As soon as I opened the door, I knew she didn't come to talk. She had three big-boy girls with her. "Where yo mama at?"

"I dunno. She left."

"Go tell Miko to come here." I turned to get Miko, but she was already coming down the stairs. Auntie Shawn smiled. "Damn, you look like King."

She walked up to Miko and hugged her.

"My daddy told me to tell you, 5-17-00."

Auntie Shawn looked at me. "Nephew, where the safe at?"

I took her to where the safe was located in my daddy's closet. When she popped it open, all I saw was money and white bricks. It was jewelry, some papers, and two guns on the top shelf.

"Nephew, go pack your shit! We leaving." I ran to find Miko, but she was already gone.

I been with my Auntie Shawn ever since. She saw how homesick I was, so she packed up and moved to Chicago. I still attend the same school. I also still got that backpack full of money and my pops phone.

Auntie Shawn is doing big things. She is always on the go and is barely at home. She still be on my ass though, making sure I don't miss a day of school.

She told me when that when I turned fifteen, it's gonna be time to pick up where my daddy left off. Hell, I'll be fifteen in four months.

"Hello! Earth to Young Meech! Nigga, where you go?"

I had to laugh. Lil Man's ass is crazy. He holding up really good. His brother and sister both got killed about a month or two ago.

"My nigga, did you ever find out who killed Pancho or TuTu?" He shook his head.

"I know who killed Pancho. I think TuTu's boyfriend killed her. I just can't prove it right now."

"Who killed Pancho?" Why did I even ask this ole extra ass nigga this shit in public? He starts breathing all hard and looking ugly in the face.

"These hoes killed him."

"Some hoes?"

"Yeah bro, it's four of them. He put them on a money lick and they killed him after they got the bread."

"Damn! That's fucked up!"

"I'm chilling for the moment, getting my money right, but when they least expect it, I'mma murk all they asses."

Seeing it was a touchy subject, I let it go. "Ah, let's go see what my Auntie into. She's back in town."

4 ~ Auntie Shawn

"Hello."

"Wake yo ass up. We got moves to make."

"Yeah, yeah. Give me an hour."

"Hour my ass! I'll be there in thirty minutes."

Damn! I hate this early morning bullshit, but when my bitch calls, I go running. I've been in love with that hoe money since I was young as fuck. That bitch be calling me. My big brother King put me on to that life. I miss him so much; my heart hurts. Losing him was like losing a part of my soul. At least I got the best part of him. Young Meech looks identical to what King used to look like.

I remember when King brought that street shit into my young world; I was like ten. I was coming from school one day and I wanted to go to the candy store. It was too dangerous for me to walk home from school by myself, but since I had my friends with me, I was good.

Back in the day, Gary, Indiana was known as the murder capital. My mommy was like so many of the other mothers in the hood…addicted to something. Heroine happened to be her drug of choice. Needless to say, she was never around to perform her motherly duties.

. It was never any food in the fridge, any heat in the winter, or hot water in the house. King knew at a young age that if he didn't hit the streets, he wouldn't eat. He was five years older than I was, and let me tell you, he was a beast in them streets.

Anyway, it was warm on this particular day, so we decided not to ride the bus. We walked down Broadway Avenue to 7th Avenue, made a left, and headed to a street named Rhode Island.

"There goes my brother's car, Carmen. I'm about to go get some money from him so we can go to the candy store. You coming?" Carmen was looking as if she saw a ghost. "What's yo problem, Carmen?"

"My brother Tank said I can't come around here. He said niggaz be dying over here, and if he caught me around here, he was gonna fuck me up." I laughed at her scared ass. "I'll be waiting on the corner with Tanya."

Quiet as kept, I felt that something wasn't right when I walked off and saw that none of my friends followed me. I walked through the gangway to the side door. Before I could knock, I heard my brother talking.

"Do what the fuck you gon do, pussy! I ain't never scared! I wasn't gon never be shit anyway!"

My heart was beating so hard that I could have sworn that whomever was in the house heard it.

"Where the rest of the dope, nigga? I'm about to shoot yo ass!"

That did something to me. My brother was in danger! He was all I had and I'd be damned if I was about to lose him. It was as if the whole damn block must have sensed the storm brewing because, all of a sudden, there wasn't a soul outside. I looked back to the corner where my friends were supposed to be and they were all gone.

Surprisingly, I was ready. I put my book bag down and crept through the open door. I wanted to cry as soon as I stepped in the kitchen. My brother's pit bull, Gucci, was laying on his side, dead! "Oh no, Gucci!" I loved that dog.

Slowly, I walk to where I heard the voices. I peeked around the corner and saw that King was on his knees with his best friend Tank lying next to him in a puddle of blood. It was two dudes with mask covering their faces standing over them.

King must have sensed an extra presence because when I peeked around the corner again, our eyes connected. I almost cried because he dropped his head.

"The money is in the laundry room." One of the dudes walked off to the laundry room. The one holding King and Tank at gunpoint laughed. "Yo ass ain't as tough as the streets say you are. You a pussy and I'mma enjoy killing you."

I started to panic I had to do something before he killed my brother. I looked around the kitchen for something. On the table, there was a bunch of powder stuff, money, and oh shit, *A GUN!*

I didn't think twice before I grabbed it. I crept back to where they were. I peeked around the corner and what I saw next will forever be embedded in my memory. King was still on his knees staring at me with tears falling from his eyes. I had never seen him cry.

I showed him that I had the gun in my hand. He smiled. "Fuck you smiling at, pussy? Yo ass 'bout to die."

King's next words were for me and I knew it. "SHOOT!"

Dude with the gun looked at him and smiled. "That's what I'm talking about. Die with some dignity."

He went to raise his gun as I was raising mine. All I was thinking to myself was, *"You better not miss."*

BOOM!

The kick from the gun knocked me flat on my back. I heard the other dude say, "What the fuck?" He saw me and charged towards me. Before I could raise the gun back up, Gucci jumped up and fought for me with his last breath. The grip he had on the man's arm was so nasty, that you could actually hear the bones in his arm breaking.

"GET THIS MOTHERFUCKING DOG!"

King ran in the room and shot the dude in his head. As he fell to the floor, Gucci let go of his arm and limped over to me where he put his head in my lap.

"King, help me get him to the doctor!" He rubbed Gucci's head and then he closed his eyes with his hand. "Come on, he's gone."

I looked down, and sure enough, he was gone. King ran in the backroom and came back holding Tank. "Shawn, go in the laundry room and grab that bag outta the dryer! Hurry up!"

I did what I was told and ran outta that house with my brother. Turns out, when I shot the gun, I missed. The noise made the gunman turn around and when he did, King knocked his lights out. Point blank, I saved his life, and from that day forward, he had my back. I no longer rode the school bus.

We took Tank to the hospital in East Chicago, Indiana and rode around for a few hours.

"What the fuck made you come to the spot?"

"I wanted five dollars for some candy."

He laughed. "I'm glad yo ass wanted some money because you saved my life. Shit, you and Gucci!"

I grew sad all over again. That was some brave shit. "I'mma miss Gucci."

From that day on, he gave me five dollars every day. He let me come chill at his spots. I watched everything.

Tank recovered and was back doing his thing. He never let Carmen come around though. He didn't want me there either, but King was the boss. "Man, take her lil ass home. This grown folks business."

Tank had a nasty disposition about him. I never trusted him.

"She saved both of our lives, so she stays. If you got a problem, you can move out." I always watched Tank. I even told King that I didn't trust him. King shoulda listened.

Now I have taken over where he left off, even as a father. I'm raising my nephew because King's baby mama and Tank decided that his life wasn't worth living.

I see that fire in my nephew's eyes. He almost ready and I'mma make sure I teach him everything. When he gets his mind and money right, we gon go find Tank.

"Don't call my phone no more, nigga! I'm up!" I hung up the phone and fired up a blunt. I been thinking about King's daughter, Miko. She dipped on me that night and I haven't been able to find her. I don't know why she didn't come with me. My phone rang once more. That shit was really starting to piss me off.

"Houston, we got a problem."

"What fool?"

"Remember that chick yo brother introduced us too?"

"The pretty redbone, Boo? The thick one? What about her?

"We really need to get up with her. She got that shit for the low-low. King always said she was 'bout that money."

"Well shit, not no more. Somebody shot her. She outta there!"

"DAMN!"

5 ~ Auntie Boo

BEEP! BEEP! BEEP!
All I can hear is machines beeping all around me. It's dark and I'm cold. *Where the fuck am I?*

I'm so tired and the more I fight against this force that's drawing me to this light, the more it hurts. When I don't resist, it feels so good. It's dark, but I can feel another presence. I look down and I see this hand gently grab my wrist. I look back up and I look into the eyes of my mother.

"Ma, I miss you so much!"

She smiles. "Then come with me. It'll stop hurting."

I start walking with her because I didn't want her to leave. "When I walk this way, it don't hurt. What's that light over there?"

"Heaven."

I let go of her hand and stop. "Heaven? Ma, I can't go yet. Lil Mama is in trouble. My dad needs me. I can't go."

She smiled again. "Life is full of pain. Come with me to paradise."

Reality set in. I need to go back. I started backing away from her. "I love you ma, but I'm not done on earth yet."

She looked at me and this time, her smile was gone. "If you go back, you'll burn."

I chuckled. "Excuse my language, but I got hell to deliver to a few people that deserve it."

"You may not be able to come back." She turned away. "Heaven is peaceful; hell is hot! Please come with me!"

I took my time before I spoke. "I'm about to send that nigga to hell that shot me and if I end up there with him, I'mma kill his ass again!" I turned away and began the painful walk back to life. As I got closer to the darkness, I could hear voices.

"What's happening to her? Why is she shaking? Go get the fucking doctor! Boo, can you hear me? If you can hear me sis, squeeze my hand."

I knew it was Lil Mama. I just couldn't do what she was asking me to do. My whole body started hurting.

"Boo, please wake up, sis! I got you!"

I felt a burst of energy that shot my ass through the darkness like a rocket.

"Oh my goodness, get the doctor! Her eyes are open!"

6 ~ Lil Mama

When I tell you that somebody is gonna die for shooting my sister, you better believe me! This has been the longest two weeks ever! After the paramedics told me that she was DOA, I blacked out. When I came to, I was lying in a hospital bed by my damn self. After a few hours of I.V. fluids and rest, I was discharged. I was nearly to my car when a paramedic called me.

"Miss, can I have a word with you?" I walked with him for a few seconds before he blurted out, "She's not dead!"

I stopped dead in my tracks. "WHAT? Now you told me---"

"I know what I told you. Just listen, okay. She was very much dead at the scene, but on the drive to the hospital, we worked our butts off to revive her."

I was on the verge of fainting, so he walked me to a set of benches outside the hospital. "I must say that your sister is a fighter."

I smiled and said, "Yeah, she is tough! I knew she wouldn't leave me." Now it was his turn to smile.

"No-no, you misunderstood me. She's a fighter because when we shocked her with the machine, she jumped up and hit me in my damn eye. See, look!"

He turned to the left, and sure enough, he had a nice black eye. I fell down laughing. "Well, where is she? I need to see her."

He grabbed my arm so tight, I was about to hit his ass in the other eye. "LET ME GO! WHAT'S--"

"Hold on, this is where it gets tricky. I could lose my job. Before she fell into a coma, she told the head doctor and me to call her dad and for us to not tell anyone else. I only told you because you acted a damn fool on the scene. No disrespect."

That shit pissed me the hell off. How come I couldn't know? I'm about to get to the bottom of this shit. "Okay, thank you."

As soon as I was behind the wheel of my car, I was calling Mr. Sheridan.

"Hey Ma, I was waiting for you to call me."

I had to calm down because I was on fire. "How come she didn't want me to know?"

"Hello? Lil Mama, you there?"

"Yeah pops, I'm here. How come---"

"You know I don't do these phones. Come to the fifth floor and wait in the waiting room."

"Ain't that the maternity ward?"

"Girl, what the hell I say?"

"Yes sir."

Ten minutes later, I was standing at the foot of Boo's bed in tears. If she ain't dead, she sho' do look like it. Whoever did this, fucked her up. Her once long, shiny black hair is matted to her head with blood still in it. "Damn, y'all couldn't fucking get the blood out of her hair? What the fuck, man?"

Pops shook his head. "That's why she didn't want yo crazy ass up here. I'm going downstairs to make some phone calls. I'll be back."

I was exhausted. I sat down next to her and put my head on her hand. "Boo, I love you sis. Please get up. We got a city to take over. Yeah chick, I know you back down. Fuck it then, me too! Let's show these niggaz who run the Chi! I need you. JuJu and her lil go-getters ready. Jaw and Poohman ready. We just need our Queen of the City. I love---"

The next thing I know, all of the machines in the room begin to go crazy.

"What the fuck? What's happening to her? Why is she shaking? Somebody go get the fucking doctor! Boo, can you hear me? If you can, squeeze my hand...NOTHING!

Damn, I'mma keep talking to her. "Boo, please wake up sis! I got you!"

Just when I was about to have an anxiety attack, her eyes popped open. "OH MY GOODNESS, GET THE DOCTOR! HER EYES ARE OPEN!" This bitch 'bout to make the city bleed!

LJ

Man Joe, these last two weeks been hell for me. I lost my Auntie and we still ain't laid her to rest. Ain't heard from nobody on her behalf. Poohman out the hospital and we definitely back on these streets letting niggaz know ain't shit sweet. Niggaz thought since we was going through something, they didn't have to run us our bread...A LIE!

As far as Ju and her lil partners in crime, we been on they asses. School and the crib. Ju know I ain't playing with her punk ass. After that bullshit we just went through, I'll die if something happens to her. ReRe living with Poohman a few blocks away. Dirty and Tiki live in the same building that me and Ju live in, so she always down there when I'm trapping.

Today has been a good day. "Ah Poohman?"

He looked at me with a mouth full of fries. "What nigga?"

"Yo old hungry ass. You look like a chipmunk!"

"Fuck you dude! I'm hungry!"

"Ole fat cheek ass nigga!"

"Why yo punk ass worried about me? You need to be worry about a new connect. We got like two bricks left."

"I ain't forgot. It's just so much shit been going on."

Before my auntie got shot, she put me on to this new connect named Shawn. Turns out, he was a she and she was looking for a new connect, so we was shit outta luck. After she found a connect, she plugged us in too and we just go through her. Fine by me. My mind been all fucked up. I'm not in no position to do shit but look stupid.

"While you was out of it Poohman, I hooked up with Shawn and got up with this new dude."

Poohman gave me the ugliest look. It was so ugly that I had to laugh. "You know I hate fucking with new niggaz, Jaw…"

"Well me too, but we going through her. She good."

There go that ugly ass face again. "Nigga, stop looking at me and just talk."

"Fuck yo porch monkey looking ass. Anyway, I'm not feeling new people, period! Other than our family, I don't trust a soul, my dude. I'm all paranoid and shit. Ask ReRe. Last night she got ready to go piss and I put her ass in a chokehold."

I began cracking up.

"Nigga, I'm serious. I almost choked her ass out."

I'm laughing so hard that I can barely see.

"I know Re's crazy ass got you back, right?"

"Hell yeah, she did. She snatched away from me and went to the bathroom. When I got good and somewhat relaxed, her crazy ass hit me in my shit so hard, I ain't even gon lie, I wanted to pistol whip her. I went to grab my pistol and this bitch pulled it from behind her and gon say, "Looking for this?" All I could do was tell her that I was sorry."

Shaking my head I ask, "Did she forgive you?"

"Hell naw! She made me ride the couch."

I'm nearly falling out the seat now laughing.

"You ain't shit Jaw! That shit ain't funny!"

"Call me what you want. You forgot that girl got bodies under her belt?"

"I ain't scared of her nigga! I'm cautious."

My phone started ringing. "Lil Mama, what's good, sexy?" My hands began shaking so bad that I had to pull over. I'm a grown ass man, but right there at that moment, I started bawling like a baby for like two minutes, at least.

"Man bro, what's wrong?"

If it were any other woman other than Boo and my Mom Dukes, I wouldn't be crying like this. Shit, I got an image to uphold, but this was my baby. "Lil Mama said meet her at Rush."

"Who the fuck up there?"

"Man, Boo alive bro!" This crazy bastard stuck his leg over to the driver side and stomped on my foot.

"DRIVE NIGGA!"

JuJu

Man, I'm so glad that Jaw's ass is gone. For the last couple of weeks, he been in my ass like a thong. I'm only allowed to go to school and the crib. I mean, damn! I can handle myself pretty much. Y'all read part one, "The Come Up" didn't you? If you didn't, then you sleeping on ya girl."

My besties and I been doing big things. We're kinda at a standstill right now. My God Mom, Boo died almost three weeks ago. That shit right there almost killed my Auntie's spirit. Lil Mama and Jaw been in their own lil world.

The initial shock of it has worn off. The show must go on. There is money to be made. After school, we been stacking out a few banks, and have two on our radar.

We all meet up at McDonald's on 79th and Yates in the mornings before we head off to school. The plan is to hit both banks at the same time. ReRe and I gon hit the one on 79th and Stony Island, and Dirty and Tiki gon hit the one on 71st and Jeffery.

I know what you thinking, but let me explain. We're sticking to the same M.O. We're following the manager's home. In the morning, we grab them from there and ride to the bank with them. Fool proof plan, right? Only problem is, we gotta shake Jaw and

Poohman's stalking asses. They think they know our schedules, but we got a trick for they asses though.

Damn, my phone's ringing. Where the fuck is it? "Hello? Hellooooo?" I hung up. I've been getting prank calls for the last few weeks. Bet not be some hoe that Jaw is creeping with. I'mma slit that nigga's throat.

"Ju, let's go get something to eat. I'm hungry." I looked at Dirty laying across the floor like a throw rug with freckles. She was high as a kite. "Yo ass fucked up!"

I started laughing because this fool was laying on the floor with her arms behind her head as if she was about to make snow angels. Maybe that ain't funny, but when you high off contact it is!

"Come on hoe; let's see if Tiki and Re wanna go. I want Fred and Jack's on 76th."

7 ~ Young Meech

Things been slow around the crib. All I been doing is going to school, chilling with Lil Man's weird ass, and then going back to the crib. "Ah Lil Man, let's make a move. I'm hungry."

"Aight, let's go to my favorite spot on 76th and Vincennes."

I looked at his ass as if he was dumb. "How we gon get there, genius? We ain't got no car."

"Man, yo Auntie got the Range in the garage. I can drive."

"Yo short ass can't drive. Remember the car you stole and tore up?"

He started laughing. "That wasn't my fault. The police was chasing me."

I thought about it for a minute. I was hungry as hell. "I'm driving."

Boo

My whole body feels like it is on fire. Everything hurts. I guess that lets me know that I'm alive. I turned my head to the left and I saw Lil Mama standing there crying. "Yo ass always crying. Ole crybaby ass lil girl."

"Bitch, fuck you! I thought you was gone. The city was about to feel my pain."

"Calm down, killa! We gon definitely make a few niggaz and bitches pay!" I turned my head the other way and closed my eyes. Physically I hoped I was ready to put that work in. The nigga I'm going after got the city on lock.

"Boo, who did this to you?"

"I can't say right now. All I can say is we gon have to come with it. I wonder if Jaw got up with that new connect. We gon have to lay low. Dude that shot me ain't gon stop till he know's I'm a distant memory."

"Shit sis! Quiet as kept, I got them lil badass kids of ours 'bout to knock off two banks at the same time."

I looked at her as if she was crazy.

"Before you say anything, everything is good. They not going in there like I did, so relax."

"Okay bitch, that's on you. Make sure they okay. Do Jaw and Poohman know?"

"Hell naw and you gon keep ya mouth closed."

"Aight, we gotta get our ducks in a row because bitch, we 'bout to tear this city up! Call Pete. We need him to find somebody."

I got ready to pick up the phone when Jaw and Poohman burst through the door like the damn police. "Jaw, what the hell, boy?"

He walked over to my bed, collapsed on it, and cried. "I'm good, baby. Stop crying." He only held me tighter. I looked up to see Lil Mama and Poohman crying too.

"Okay, okay, dry y'all motherfucking eyes!" I rubbed Jaw's dreads and lifted his head with my hand. "Look at me." He did. "It's time to put yo murder game down!"

"Yeah Auntie, let's do this. I got at the connect. She said whenever you ready, but who did this to you?"

"I'mma put you up on game in due time. In the meantime, let's get this money because come the New Year, I want us some place other than Chicago. This city 'bout to be turned upside down. We ain't got no choice but to leave after that." I couldn't believe what I was saying...leave Chicago. My home. I don't know shit else. Fuck it! I can make new memories elsewhere.

"Jaw, call Shawn and meet with her. Get what you can get and move that shit in a week. You still got them trap spots?"

"We just opened two more."

"Good, now let's make them moves. Lil Mama, call the doctor. I need to know how long before I can be discharged."

Lil Man

"Man Joe, this mafucka ride smooth as fuck! Let me drive."

"No nigga." Young my homie, but he be acting like a pussy sometimes. I been on my grind. His Auntie gave us some shit to move and that's exactly what we did. That lil money came in handy. I been getting my gear intact. I can't pull no bitches looking like a bum. I just turned fourteen three days ago, so you know I'm feeling myself.

I been creeping through the hood looking for them Eastside Crazy Bitches. Whenever I see those hoes, I'm dumping on they asses. I found out through JuJu's lil cousin that they did kill my brother. She been trying to be my girl for a minute now. I play lil mind games with her to keep her close.

I'm supposed to meet up with her tomorrow night. I got something for that lil bitch. She can thank her cousin for the pain and suffering that she's going to endure.

"Earth to Lil Man!"

"Aw damn Young, my bad. What you say?"

"I asked what you want from here?"

"Get me a cheeseburger with fries and a vanilla milkshake."

"Aight."

I turned on the radio and my shit, "Big Daddy by Nicki Minaj and Meek Mills was playing. *"Yo bitch, call me Big Daddy. Tell that bitch, I'm Big Daddy."*

I started bobbing my head to the beat when I thought I saw a ghost. "What the fuck?" I picked up the phone and called Big Moe.

"What up lil nigga?"

"I see all four of them bitches up here at Fred and Jack's"

"You got yo pistol?"

"Hell yeah."

"Then what you waiting for? Air they asses out! Call me when it's done!"

"Aight." I reached under the passenger seat and got my gun. I checked the clip and put one in the chamber. "This for Pancho, bitches!"

I jumped out the truck and ran to the entrance. I couldn't believe my eyes. Young was hugging one of them bitches. "Fuck it! He can get it too!" I closed my eyes and let that thang bark!

Tiki

Man, everything is all weird and shit. We just tryna keep our head above water. In a few days, we about to hit two banks at the same time. Yeah, we 'bout that life. We been sneaking around since Ju's lil boyfriend been stalking us.

"Re, call them bitches. I'm hungry."

"Dirty just called and said come downstairs. They going to Fred and Jack's."

"Good because my stomach is in my damn back."

We jumped in the car with JuJu and Dirty E, and as always, its weed all in the air. "If we get pulled over, they gon take yo car, dummy."

E smiled and said, "We got the bread to get it back, now shut the fuck up, and hit this dummy."

"You don't know me nigga! Pass that shit, then!"

We started cracking up. As we were pulling up in the parking lot, I saw this raw ass Range Rover. "I want one of those."

JuJu turned around and burst my bubble. "You got the money, go ahead and the FEDS gon pop yo ass, bitch!"

I was clueless. "How you figure?"

"If you spend more than $10,000 on a car and you don't have any proof of where that money came from, yo ass hit."

"I'mma go over on Western where them Arabs at. They take cash."

"Since you think you so gah damn smart, tell me why they just got hit by the FEDS? You can holla at them in about seven to ten years! Where you been?"

"Damn!"

We jumped out the car on a mission. As we were standing in line waiting for our food, this lil nigga walked up to me. He got all the way up in my face as if he knew me. "Damn shorty, can I help you?" I almost passed out when I got a better glance.

"Tell me yo name is Miko."

"MEECH?"

Oh my stars! This is my little brother! "WHERE…WHAT…HOW?"

"I been looking for you for years, Miko!"

He picked me up and spun me around. "Boy, put me down!" I was laughing and crying at the same time. "Damn boy! You look just like daddy!" I just couldn't believe that I was staring at my lil brother.

JuJu grabbed him by the arm and hugged him too. "You got so big, Meechie!" He looked at Ju and smiled. He always had a crush on her. "What up Ju?"

I was beyond happy to see him. "Who you up here with?"

"I drove Auntie's truck up here with my lil homie from the hood. He in the car on the phone."

I was about to say something else when I saw this nigga running up to the door with his gun pointed directly at us.

"MEECH! GET DOWN!" I snatched his arm on the way to the ground.

BOC! BOC! BOC! BOC! BOC!

What the fuck? "E, get this nigga off us!"

Dirty grabbed her gun and crawled to the door. As soon as the shooter stopped, Dirty started.

BOOM! BOOM! BOOM! BOOM!

Shit just got real! E shooting, this nigga shooting, and we are all helpless on the ground. Meechie snatched away from me and jumped up.

"MEECHIE NOOO!"

Fuck what I was saying, he pulled out this big ass Glock 40 and pointed it at the nigga who was now running away and let him have it.

BOC! BOC! BOC! BOC! BOC!

"STOP SHOOTING! THE POLICE ON THE WAY! I HEAR THE SIRENS! LET'S GO!"

"Meech, let's go!"

"Sis, I hit that nigga! I heard him scream!"

"Go get Auntie's truck and meet us on 84th and Marquette!"

I looked around at what used to be my favorite fast food spot. "Damn y'all, we gotta go; look." It was dead bodies everywhere.

"Y'all better hurry up before we get blamed for this shit."

As we were running to the car, it didn't dawn on me that we didn't check for security cameras. "I hope they don't have no cameras."

8 ~ Lil Man

"**M**an Big Moe, take me to the hospital. This shit hurts!"

"Fuck naw! I'mma take you to Leaks and Sons on 79th."

I looked at this nigga as if he was crazy. "Why the fuck you taking me to a funeral home for? I ain't dead!"

He had the nerve to look at me and smile. "Yo ass will be if you don't get that bullet removed from that hole. Who shot you?"

"Man, I dunno. I had they asses too. All of them scary ass hoes hit the floor." I had to laugh at myself because my adrenaline was still pumping. That shit was so crazy I pissed my pants. "What's going on? Come on, fuck. I'm bleeding, asshole."

"Shut yo lil punk ass up. It's a shoulder wound lil crybaby ass nigga."

Shoulder wound or not, my shit hurts. I got a million thoughts running through my head. Why was Meech hugging one of them hoes? Where he know them from? Is that nigga plotting on me? I'mma get to the bottom of this shit. I'm killing everybody. Damn, I'm getting lightheaded.

SMACK! SMACK!

"Don't pass out in my shit lil nigga, we here!"

Young Meech

What's really going on? I been calling Lil Man's phone all damn day and he's not answering. When I got back in the truck after the shooting, he was gone. I'm happy as shit I found my sister, but I'm worried about my dude.

"Damn! It's a fucking bullethole in this lady's truck!"

My phone started ringing. Why the hell did it have to be my Auntie? "Hey Auntie."

"Hey Auntie, my ass! Where you at with my truck, boy?"

"You not gon believe this. I found Miko." It was quiet for a few seconds. I knew her lil tough ass was crying. "Auntie, you heard me?"

"Is she okay? Where she at?"

"We had a minor problem at Fred and Jack's, but we cool."

"Minor problem? What happened?"

"Man Auntie, some nigga shot up the restaurant."

"WHAT?"

"We cool. Dirty and me got his ass up off us. I hit him in the back."

"With what gun? You got that gun outta yo daddy's bag, didn't you?"

"Yes, ma'am."

"Where y'all at now?"

"On the way to Miko's house on 84th and Marquette."

"I'll meet you there."

JuJu

I don't know why we are always in the line of fire. We ain't did shit to nobody, I don't think. We been laying low, so why are niggas shooting at us?

"JuJu, where was you just at girl?"

"My bad E, you know I gotta tell Jaw about this."

E shook her head. "Don't do that. Yo ass gon be under lock and key for real."

On some real shit, we need to go on and hit them banks before shit gets real. Things been wild around here. My Auntie Lil Mama been on another planet. That situation with Boo got her stressing. Money has got to be made around here, feel me? And we are gonna be the ones to make it!

When we got to Tiki's crib, we all hopped out with caution. "E, grab that bag outta the trunk." As always, her mouth is on point with the slick shit.

"Fuck wrong with yo hands?"

"Do what I said and come the hell on."

Once we got to the crib, we got down to business. "Okay look, we need to go ahead with our plans ASAP. I overheard Jaw and Poohman's conversation and they got something big going on in like a week. I heard they was about to get a big shipment coming in. I think some real shit is about to go down. We gon need the need the extra bread to have their backs. Y'all with it?"

ReRe was in deep thought so I got to her first. "Re, what's good?"

"I'm worried that Poohman is going to get hurt again."

"Aww girl, shake that shit off. That nigga a goon."

Just as I was about to go in on her, Tiki's lil brother walked in. "How you know what house to go to?"

"I showed him." My little cousin Tyesha walked in with a smile on her face. "He pulled up and he looked lost so I asked him if he needed some help."

I looked at him with a smirk. "And let me guess, you wanted to All-State assist his ass, didn't you?"

"Whatever cuz."

Meech stepped up with a big ass smile on his face. "What up y'all? What I miss?"

I thought about it for a minute. "Tiki let me holla at you for a minute." We dipped off to the other room. She looked at me with this 'Un—Uh bitch' look. "What you thinking Bitch?"

"You saw how yo brother handled himself at the restaurant? We can use the extra muscle."

"Damn Ju, I don't know if he into that shit. I just barely saw him."

"If he toted a pistol, he into something."

She thought about it for a second. "Yeah, you right. I'mma see what he about."

We headed back into the living room and the first thing I saw was Tyesha and Meechie all boo'ed up on the couch. "Aw yeah lil cuz, let me find out."

We been on good terms ever since I started making money. Her mama, my auntie, is still a hoodrat. I make sure her gear is right. I also stopped her from fucking with them niggaz and she is still in school. I'm on that ass. So to see her flirty with someone her own age is kinda cute.

"Tiki, holla at Meech. Tyesha, come on, let's go find us some business."

Auntie Shawn

"Let me know what time you gon be ready. I need that ASAP!"

Damn, being in the game is hard. It's always something. I'm dying to see my niece. I been thinking about her for years, always wondering where she was. It's time to think about another career. This shit ain't gon be my life. While driving through the streets of Chicago, I begin to miss my brother. He was that nigga. I'mma make it my business to find and kill the nigga that took him from me.

I'mma find that bitch ass nigga, Tank too. Word around town is that Tank had his nephew kill my brother. I'mma do my homework before I make it rain on these streets and I'm not talking 'bout no fucking hundreds.

RING! RING!

"Yeah, Meech? I'm around the corner, what's up?"

"I dunno. Have Lil Man been around the house?"

"I ain't seen him. Why?"

"I can't say, but something ain't right."

"I'm in front of the house now, tryna find a parking spot. MEECHIE, WHAT THE HELL? IS THAT BULLET HOLES IN MY FUCKING TRUCK?"

"Auntie, let me explain."

"EXPLAIN MY ASS! BOY, I"MMA KILL YOU!"

CLICK!

9 ~ Detective House

"What do we have here?"

"Well, from what we see, it looks like a robbery gone bad. We got three victims over here, all dead from gunshot wounds to the back...execution style. The cashier took two to the face. The poor cook took four to the back and fell face first on the hot grill. I think we're going to need dental to identify him."

"Damn! This is a fucking massacre. I know this is going to put a halt to my operation take down of the Eastside Crazy Crew. Shit! Are there any surveillance cameras?"

"Actually there is. The other officer is in the back there now reviewing them."

I stepped over the cook and almost threw up. It smelled like burnt shit up in here.

"Officer Dixon, what we got here?"

"I'm almost there. I'm trying to rewind it to the time of the first 911 call. Hold on. Okay, here we go. At 1:35 p.m., four people came in and placed their orders. At 1:41 p.m., this white Range Rover pulled up in the parking lot and the driver exited the vehicle and entered the establishment. Apparently, the driver knew the four individuals that entered several minutes before him."

"How do you know that?"

"Look at the camera footage from the lobby. The driver picked up one of the females and hugged her."

"WAIT! Pause the footage."

"House, what do you see?"

"The briefing we had this morning about operation takedown. Well, those are my perps."

"No shit!"

"No shit. Play it."

"Okay, well this is where things get crazy."

"How so?"

"Well, the Range Rover has another passenger. After about three minutes or so, he exits the Range with what appears to be a gun in his right hand. He runs up to the door and starts firing."

"On his boy?"

"I know, right. On the lobby footage, you can see bodies dropping and your perps dive for cover. Whomever this girl is to him, he did his best to cover her. Look at this young man jump up and return fire."

"Damn! These mafuckas decided to have a shootout in broad daylight."

"Well, the driver jumped up and helped the other guy return fire."

"So now the driver is shooting at the passenger that he came with?"

"Yup. After about seven seconds, the passenger backs off and makes a run for a black SUV."

"Aw shit! Did I just see him go down?"

"I think so. Wait let me rewind it. Yup, he was shot on his way to the SUV."

I had to shake my head for a second. "Do you know who shot him?"

"Wait; let me look at the lobby footage. Damn!"

"What?"

"From the looks of things, his friend shot him."

"I'mma need some help with this one. Care to assist me?"

Officer Dixon was a bad chick. She was from Detroit, Michigan. I love her swag. She is a tomboy, but I can tell she had a badass body under them clothes. Lawd have Mercy! She has a beautiful face with some very sharp cheekbones. Skin smooth as caramel, with these deep dark eyes.

"Are you flirting with me detective?"

I had to smile. "Yes, but I could really use your help on this one."

"I'll be more than glad to help you, but let's be clear on one thing."

"What's that?"

"I like what you like."

"And that is?"

"Pussy!"

Damn, she shut a nigga down real quick. She is a damn good cop though. I read her jacket. She came from a broken home. Her father, mother, and sister were all murdered after she took down a big drug lord in Detroit some years ago and came to Chicago to start over.

"Well, I see you did your homework on me. I would love to assist you. Just keep your hands to yourself. This is strictly business. I'm not that kinda girl."

"You got it. I'mma get in touch with my informant. I just need a positive I.D. on these four here."

"Well, what are we going to do about this? Clearly it's a case of self-defense on their end."

"We won't do shit for now. I should be able to find out who that young man is through my informant."

"Okay, well let me finish up in here and we can leave."

10 ~ LJ

Shit been crazy for the last two weeks. Poohman and I got up with Shawn and got a few bricks for a damn good price. I was impressed. Poohman and I been in them streets nonstop tryna get this money in order. Boo's been laying low. I check in with her daily, but for the most part she don't want nobody to know where she at.

I been in and out of the crib, barely seeing my baby JuJu. She ain't been tripping on a nigga being gone either. That made my antennas go up. "Ah Poohman, them lil mafuckas up to something again."

He stopped counting his money and took a deep pull on his blunt. "Aww shit Jaw. I don't wanna hear that shit. Why you say that?"

"JuJu been real pleasant with a nigg."

"What's wrong with that? Shit, Re been real nice to me. Shit, I finally got the pussy."

I had to laugh at that because JuJu finally let me slide into some of that. And I'll be damned... She was a virgin. That just made me love her ass even more. "I'mma fuck her and them three lil bastards up because I know deep in my heart that they on some bullshit."

"Man Joe, I can't get this money with a clear mind knowing that they are up to something that could potentially get them hurt."

"Let me call Ice and Drop. They could run the spots for us."

I thought about it for a minute. "Poohman, I swear I'mma kick this girl's ass if she ain't doing what she supposed to be doing."

Damn! Here we go again with this bullshit!

(3 Weeks Later)

As I suspected, these lil mafuckas was on some crazy shit. They're plotting on robbing two banks. All I could do was shake my head. Poohman and I have been on some stalking shit again. We've been following they asses., and from what we been seeing, they got their shit down packed.

"Poohman, should we let them go through with this? I don't want a repeat of last time."

"Hell, a part of me wanna see if they got it in em."

I wanted to punch the fuck outta this fool. "You like that shit don't you?"

"Nigga yo ass done got soft. They was robbing shit before we met them. To be honest with you, had we not ran up in that bank, I think they woulda made it up outta there. Re had that big ass AK-47 and was not afraid to use it. For real my nigga, if we planning on shutting the city down, we need them on turn up mode. Let that soft shit go. Just have her back like I got Re's"

"You right. I still wanna see how they gon pull this shit off."

JuJu

"Tiki, we 'bout to make that move in exactly three days."

"Why three days?"

"I dunno, I just think we been sitting on it too long. We know everything to a T! Now that your brother and his friend are on board, we are going to be extra tight. He said his friend is 'bout that business, but he ain't heard from him since the shooting. I hope he aight. We could use the extra muscle."

After going over a few more details, Tiki went home and I got my lazy ass up and made my boo something to eat. We been together for almost five months now and it's been the shit. I finally gave him the pooh-pooh kat and now this nigga been all in my ass. I know I got that good-good.

After putting the finishing touches on the steak and potatoes I had prepared, I went to go jump in the shower. I turned on the radio to my favorite station, WGCI. Late night love was on. "Aww shit! This my jam! ♬ ♬ *I must have rehearsed my lines, a thousand times... Until I had them memorized.* ♬ ♬ "

The music was so loud that I never heard the front door open and close. As I was reaching for my dry towel, a big black figure stood before me looking as if he was ready to kill something.

"Bitch if you scream, I'mma paint the walls with your fucking brains!"

"What the fuck?" Damn! How did I let this big King Kong looking motherfucker creep up on me? "If you want some money, I don't have---"

WHACK! This nigga slapped me so hard that I saw stars.

"Lie again bitch! You got all my money and I want it back! ALL OF IT!"

I took a closer look at the figure standing before me and almost passed out. It was Big Moe!

"W-w-wait a minute. That money ain't here, Big Moe."

WHACK! He slapped me again.

"Bitch, quit saying my name like you know me. I'mma have fun killing you!"

Fuck, I'm hit. Where the fuck is Jaw's ass when I need him the most? I swear if this nigga kills me, I'mma haunt Jaw's ass forever.

SNATCH! This nigga grabbed me out the of shower by my neck as if I was a ragdoll. He tossed me on the bed and jumped on top of me. "Get yo big ass off of me! I can't breathe!"

WHACK! "You wanna talk shit, bitch? I know how to shut you the fuck up!"

He pulled out his dick and I almost fainted. It was at least ten inches. "You ain't sticking that ugly motherfucker in me!"

"You still wanna talk shit, huh?"

He stood up and pulled out his gun. That's when I knew a bitch was in trouble. "Bitch, you killed my cousin at the bank and yo auntie shot my other cousin…"

"Please don't kill me. I'll get you, your money."

He paused and thought about what I said for a few seconds. Just when I thought that he had considered what I said, he raised his gun. "You know what? Fuck that money! I can rob plenty of banks. I'mma kill every last one of you bitches starting with you."

POW!

POW!

POW!

"ARGGGGGG!"

"Damn JuJu, wake the fuck up. You scared the shit outta me. What's wrong?"

"Bitch, Big Moe tried to kill me in my dreams."

"Big Moe?"

"Yes bitch; Big Moe! Damn, that shit was too real! We need to hit them banks and lay low!"

(Somewhere Across Town)

Big Moe

"Wake yo punk ass up. You should be aight to move around. I got things to do. I'm tired of babysitting yo lil ass."

"You so damn insensitive. Nigga, I got shot!"

"And it's been three weeks. What you gon tell yo boy?"

"I'mma tell him that the niggas that shot at him, shot me. I mean, I did get shot."

This lil boy smart and stupid. "Even if he does believe that, then why did it take you three weeks to call him?"

"Because I was fucked up. He better not question me. Shit, I don't answer to nobody."

I swear, after I kill all these bitches, I'm killing his smartass mouth too. No witnesses! I looked down and saw that I had two missed calls. My phone started to ring again so I quickly answered it. "Ah yo, what up Uncle T?"

"Come see me ASAP! I think we might have a little situation that needs to be cleaned up."

"Give me 'bout an hour."

I hung up and got dressed. For as long as I could remember, my Uncle T has been in my corner. When my daddy decided to dip on my mom's before I was born, my Uncle T stepped in. My mom was moving a lot of weight for him back in the day. Something went wrong and she was found with two bulletholes in her head.

I was only three months old. My G-Ma raised me. My Uncle T was in and out of my life until I was sixteen. My G-Ma called him to come get me. The night before, I had caught my first body and she helped me cover it up.

This lil nigga named Marcus used to be on the same shit I was on...robbing niggas. One night I was laying in the cut waiting for my target to come home. I was ready to pop his ass and take all of his shit, but that punk ass nigga Marcus beat me to the punch.

I had been watching Snowman for weeks. Fuck that! He was gonna have to let me get all that. I sat back and let him do his thing. As I watched him, I grew madder and madder.

First off, he wore a mask...pussy! How you gon make these niggas fear you if you don't show 'em who you are? Then after he ran the niggas pockets, he pistol-whipped him. Who does that? Shoot that motherfucker! If you don't, he'll probably come back for you. Now I'm on fire!

As soon as he was finished, he ran right in my direction. I wanted no time when I jumped on his ass. "Man Joe, let me get all that!"

He looked at me as if he was about to lie. "Go ahead and lie so I can lay yo ass down. Matter of fact…"

BOC! BOC! BOC! I shot him three times in the chest. Then I bent down and ran his pockets. I even snatched the chain and watch that he wore. Just as I was about to make my getaway, this apartment door flew open. "Mon? Is that you? Get yo ass in here now!"

My G-Ma was downstairs playing pinochle with her old ass friends. She made me change clothes and she held on to my pistol. She was a "G" for real.

After that, she told my Uncle T that I was ready for him. He was that nigga on the streets. Boogie and Jr's mind hadn't been corrupted yet, so they stayed around G-Ma. Uncle T showed me the drug game real fast. It was aight, but robbing niggas was my thing. He turned me into the monster that I am today. Right before I turned seventeen, I caught my second body.

All that day, Uncle T and I had been riding around smoking Kush and drinking Grey Goose. My Uncle was always soft spoken and laid back, but the phone call he got that day pissed him off. I remember him saying, "Fuck you! I don't give a fuck who you are! We'll see nigga!"

When he hung up the phone, I swear I saw steam coming from his ears. Shit, I was scared to speak. He bust a U-turn and sped down 67th street. We pulled up behind this black two door Infiniti. He handed me a gun and simply said, "Kill that nigga in the car in front of us."

There was a slight hesitation in me. "I SAID SHOOT THAT NIGGA!" The coldness in his eyes chilled my blood. There was nothing else left to be said. I jumped out of the car, crept up to the driver side window, and opened fire. POP! POP!

Damn, should I shoot the lil girl too? The only reason I didn't shoot her was because she covered her eyes. I didn't find out 'til later that I had killed the *Infamous King Meech*! I'll never forget the look in his eyes when I pulled the trigger. It was as if he welcomed death. I saw no fear in him at all. That was the same look I saw in his son's eyes that day at the restaurant.

Now that I think about it, he might be a problem if he finds out that I killed his father. We'll see how that turns out for his lil ass if he tries. I'mma a killer! He better come with it if he wants me.

Back to the present. I know that I have to watch my back and I can't trust no one! "It's time for you to move the hell around. I'm tired of babysitting yo punk ass."

"I got yo punk. I'mma call a ride. Don't worry; I'll be gone by the time you get back."

He lucky I need his ass. He reminds me of a younger Boogie. Always talking shit. "Lock the door behind you, punk!"

11 ~ Lil Man

It took me three week to recover from my wound and think of a good lie to tell this nigga. I'mma get to the bottom of all this funny shit. If that nigga has anything to do with them Eastside Crazy Bitches, his ass is gonna die with them. "What up bro?"

"Nigga, where the fuck yo ass been? I got an A.P.B. out on you. Are you okay? Where the fuck did you go? Naw, fuck all that! Where are you now? I'm 'bout to slide on you."

"Slow down bro. First off, when we pulled up to the restaurant, I jumped on the phone with a lil bitch. We were going back and forth when I see this black Tahoe pull up across the street. The shit didn't feel right so I tell ole girl I'mma hit her back and I hung up. I pulled my gun from under the seat, sunk low in my seat, and waited. I was trying to see what the driver was on. Next thing I know is the passenger from the truck jumped out the truck, ran towards the store, and opened fire. My nigga, I was able to let off one shot before my gun jammed. The nigga wasn't alone. This light-skinned cat jumped out the truck and started running towards me shooting. I got ghost on his ass. As I went to hit the corner, my back started to burn. Next thing I know, I woke up in the hospital."

"Damn, why you just now calling me? Nevermind. That shit was crazy! I shot one of them niggas though. I think it was the one running. I swear I was aiming at that boy's head. Where you at? I'm 'bout to ride down on you."

I gave the nigga the address and hung up. I'll be damned. That motherfucker shot me! I'mma kill his ass too!

(20 Minutes Later)

"Bout time nigga! What's good?"

"Look like yo bony ass loss some weight."

"Hell yeah, that shit hurt like hell too. What up wit it doe?"

He looked around before he spoke. "Whose spot is this?"

"My cousin's. He's the one who picked me up from the hospital since my trifling ass mama didn't. Let's roll."

We took the elevator and walked to the parking garage.

"My nigga, who you got in the truck wit you?"

"Aw, that's my shawty, Tyesha."

I had to shake my head because this nigga did not just say *Tyesha*. "Tyesha from 88th and Marquette?"

"Yeah, how you know her?"

"I went to school wit her."

This hoe was just all in my face and now she riding that next nigga's jock! I'mma enjoy killing this bitch. After she leads me to her cousin and the rest of her friends, it's lights out. "What's good, Tyesha?"

This bitch had the nerve to not even look at me when she spoke. She was acting as if she was too good to look. "Hey, Lil Man."

I can't wait 'til I get a chance to put my hands around her neck.

"Ah my nigga, I need to holla at you about some real important shit."

"Aight, drop her off real quick so we can chop it up then."

"Naw, she good. She already know."

"SHE ALREADY KNOW? WHAT PART OF THE GAME IS THAT?"

"Chill homie, if you'd quit snapping and let a nigga talk, I could fill you in."

It took everything in me not to fuck the both of them up. The nerve of this clown. Discussing personal business in front of hoes. "Aight, go head."

"I haven't seen my sister since my daddy died a few years back."

"Yo sister?"

Yes. When we went to the restaurant, I ran into her and her three best friends that she grew up with."

"You got a sister?"

"Damn Lil Man, for real?"

"Aight, my bad."

"Anyway after the shooting, we met up at Miko's crib on 84th and Marquette. That's when I found out that they been out here doing their thing. I'm talking 'bout robbing niggas, robbing banks, and some mo shit. They got a big job coming up and they need an extra set of eyes and ears."

"What kind of job?"

"They 'bout to hit two banks at the same time."

JACKPOT! And here I thought it was gonna be hard to get close to the E.S.C. gang. I can't wait to call Big Moe. "What exactly is it that we gotta do?"

"I'm going with Miko and Dirty and you're going to watch out for JuJu and ReRe. Deal?"

I couldn't be any luckier. "Hell yeah, we got a deal. Let's get this money."

12 ~ Young Meech

Shit 'bout to get real out here, real quick. I'mma 'bout to change the game with this bank shit. I would have never thought that my big sister would be out here in some shit like this. They some goons for real! I been out here doing a lil hustling here and there. Real talk, I think my Auntie Shawn won't put me on because I hang with Lil Man's dumbass. She tolerates him because of me, but she don't trust him for real. Now that I think about it, something about his ass ain't right. I just can't put my fingers on it.

"Boo, I'm hungry." Snapping me outta my thoughts, I focused on Tyesha's cute baby face.

"My bad, love. I got a lotta shit on my mind. What you want to eat?"

"Ummm, I want a taco dinner from Pepe's."

I looked in the rearview mirror to ask the nigga Lil Man what he wanted to eat and I caught him mugging the shit outta my girl. "Who the fuck pissed in yo Cherrios, nigga?"

"My shoulder hurt. I ain't hungry. Before you hit Pepe's, drop me off at home."

"You not gon hit her cousin's crib with me so we can finalize the plans we got for the day after tomorrow?"

I could have sworn that I saw some type of look of panic on his face. "N-naw, I took some pain pills so I'm tired. Come get me by yo'self tomorrow so we can talk about it."

"Aight my dude. You sure you ain't hungry?"

"I'm good fool."

I pulled up in front of his momma's crib and jumped out so I could walk him to the door. "Lil Man, you know you my nigga, right?"

"Yeah, and you mine, so what's good?"

"I got cha back for life."

"Good looking out homie."

"I'll see you tomorrow." I walked back to the truck with a lot of thoughts in my head. My father always told me that you'll always know if a motherfucker is for you, if you say you got they back. The correct response is *I got yours too.*

"Meechie what's wrong, boo?"

I been kicking it with shorty for a little over three weeks. I been knowing Lil Man for years. Him saying that he had my back should have come naturally. I looked at Ty and tried my luck. "Even though I ain't been knowing you that long, if any bullshit ever pop off, I got yo back, boo."

She turned in her seat so that she was looking directly at me. "Meechie, I got your back too, boo. We gon ride or die together."

Damn, I should have stopped fucking with that nigga right then. Always follow your first mind.

"I like that feisty shit, girl. Let's roll out."

Dirty E

"Yo ass stupid. Put that shit down before you accidently shoot me."

I'm sitting over here with my besties and we're putting the final touches on our plans for the day after tomorrow.

"Alright, y'all already know that we moving out at 5:30 a.m."

"Why?"

"Because that will give us more than enough time to get to the bank manager's house. Tiki, when you and JuJu follow, make sure y'all keep a safe distance."

"We don't need you to tell us shit, *Ms. Know It All*. Ju and I got this. You just make sure you are where you need to be when I grab that bitch. Having the extra pair of eyes makes things a little bit better now."

In my mind, I'm thinking that we don't need no extra fucking eyes if you ask me. "Tiki, did yo brother tell y'all who his homie is? I don't believe that he did." I looked at Tiki and waited for her response.

"Naw, come to think of it, we don't know his name."

"Man Joe, check that shit out because we need everything to go as planned."

We don't need the extra bullshit this time. Thinking back to the last robbery, we made a lot of costly mistakes. I'm the man in this group and I protect my besties.

"Ah Ju, ya parole officer been lurking?"

"Fuck you, Punk! He ain't got a clue. I been real nice to him, even though I wanna kill his ass right now. Coming in the house all hours of the night like shit sweet. After we hit this lick, I'm going Kaboom on his slick ass."

I love my sisters. We are going to come out on top and as God as my witness, anybody that wanna cross us gon dance with the devil. And I love to dance!"

Auntie Boo

Damn, this gon be a long road to a healthy recovery. The bullet did a lot of nerve damage. I gotta hurry up and get well because I got two niggas to lay the fuck down; Big Moe and AH.

Me and AH grew up together. I can't lie, the nigga been a beast. He taught my big sis Heidi and I everything from slanging to banging. But, when you in them streets, it's always a possibility that you'll get hemmed up.

Well, he got knocked by the FEDS in the early 90's. Word around town is that the nigga started working with them peoples. He disappeared for a while and then resurfaced...as the fucking police! I'mma take his ass to hell with me.

KNOCK! KNOCK!

"Who the fuck is that?"

I'm so damn paranoid that I grabbed my gun and limped to the door. Nobody's supposed to know I'm here. "Yo?"

"Yo my ass. Open the door, bitch!"

"Heidi?"

"Naw hoe! It's Santa Claus."

Who the fuck told this hoe that I was here? I open the door and in comes my big sis looking like Baby D from the movie Next Friday. She has on all black with some black and white Air Max. Her hair is pulled back in a ponytail and her face was shiny as hell. I bust out in a painful laugh. "Bitch, who you 'bout to fight?"

"The question is who did I whoop?"

"Well, who did you whoop?"

"Pete!"

"Pete? The P.I.? Bitch, why?"

"First off, Lil Mama acting all stank like she can't tell me where you was. I shoulda punched her frail ass, but I knew that I woulda had to beat that skinny bitch down. I went to Pete because I know that he would know something. I get at him on some where my sister type shit. I'm worried about her. Girl, would you believe me if I said that lil creep got smart with me?"

I didn't believe that. Everybody knows that Heidi is not to be played with. I saw her knock her baby daddy out cold. "You lying bitch! Pete knows better!"

"Fuck you mean I'm lying? I am not! He gave me some attitude, and I gave him a beat down. I literally had to beat the address out of him."

I couldn't help, but laugh. Poor Pete. He's only five feet; give or take an inch. Heidi is every bit of six feet. "Bitch, you a bully. Anyway, A shot me."

She flopped down on the couch. "Damn Boo, you know we not letting that shit slide!"

"Sis, you know he's the police now."

"Fuck that Boo, he been that! I got something for his ass!"

I knew that I had to do something. Money ain't an issue. Jaw and Poohman doing their thang on the dope side.

"Earth to Boo. What's the plan?"

I just looked at that scary motherfucker. "Bitch, you'll fight. But I know you ain't busting no pistols."

"Hell naw! That's what I got my seeds for. You know what? Just because you gon need some assistance, I'mma make an exception. I'm riding with you sis!"

I just stared at her for a second. The look in her eyes let me know that she was dead serious. "That's what's up because I'mma need you."

"Get yo ass outta that wheelchair. You ain't fucked up. Let me see you move around."

"Where we going, Heidi?"

"I'm taking you to physical therapy."

"You ain't taking me nowhere looking like a big black Power Ranger."

"Oh yeah? You can go by ya damn self with yo smartass mouth!"

JoJo

I'm glad that my sister let me move in with her. It's live as shit over here. These hoes are some real haters. I'm cool with this one girl. She lives a few blocks over and her name is Tyesha. She stays fresh to death...My kinda bitch. She told me that her cousin, JuJu, takes good care of her. I can respect that. Ramone looks out for me too.

Tonight we supposed to hit the skating rink with her dude and his friend. "Hello? Ty? Where y'all at?"

"Meet us at the gas station on 83rd and Commercial."

"Okay, I'm walking out the door now."

I'm really feeling Derrick. I don't call him Lil Man. He a little weird, but I'mma fix all that. As I'm walking out the door, I run into Ramone.

"Where you think you going?"

"Out."

"With who, smartass?"

"If you really must know, I'm going to the rink with Ty, her guy, and Derrick."

"Who is Derrick?"

"You met him at the rib spot."

"That lil nigga, Lil Man?"

"Yeah, why?"

"Be home at a reasonable hour."

I tried my luck and stuck my hand out. "Can I have some money?"

"You lucky I love you."

As soon as he pulled out his bankroll, I snatched it. "Give it up, Big Daddy."

JuJu

It was Thursday night and we were bored outta our minds around this bitch. ReRe and Tiki are laid at the foot of my bed. Tiki was on her phone caking with some bitch. She was all giggly and shit. Re's ass was high as a kite. Her and Dirty had just got through smoking some purple haze.

"Y'all, I'm bored as hell."

Re rolled over to face me. "Bitch, let's relax. You know we're hitting those banks in the morning."

"So what? It's only 6 o'clock and we sitting in the crib. Let's hit the skating rink on 76th and Racine."

"The rink? Bitch, I am not twelve again."

I hit Re's ass in the head with a pillow. "Y'all hoes ain't no fun."

I kicked Tiki on her leg. "Get off the phone, lame." She flipped me off.

"Baby, I'mma see you tomorrow, okay?" She hung up the phone and kicked me back. "You a hater, Ju!"

"What am I hating on…Carpet Muncher?"

We all started laughing when E came out of the blue. "Ain't nothing wrong with munching on a little carpet."

I looked on the side of my bed and saw E laying on the floor spread out as if she was on the verge of making a few snow angels. "Why you on the floor, dummy?"

She opened her eyes and smiled. "Because y'all hoes woulda tried to take advantage of all this manliness."

I rolled my eyes. "Bitch, please! Only cat I like is my own."

"Let's roll to the rink."

"That's right E, tell Thelma and Louise let's do something."

Tiki got up from the bed and fixed her clothes. "Aight, but we coming in before 11 o'clock."

(A Few Hours Later)

We got to the rink a quarter to eight and there were so many damn kids everywhere. "E, you got your gun?"

"You know it. Why?"

"You know how these lil young niggas like to act stupid."

Re walked up to the counter and got all of us some skates. We used to hit the rinks all of the time. "Ju, ain't that Tyesha over there with Meechie cutting up on the dance floor?

I turned around and saw my lil cousin junking on Meechie. They was doing the fool. "Come on Tiki, let's go over there."

Re grabbed her skates. "Me and E about to hit a few laps."

Lil Man

I don't know whose idea it was to go skating, but I'm mad about this shit. I've got more important shit to do. I saw out of the corner of my eye that JoJo was looking at me.

"Why yo face all bawled up?"

I looked at her and smiled. "That's just how I look. What's good with you though?"

"I'm good. You gon skate a few laps and step with me?"

"I don't skate, but I'll watch you. After you finish, I'll buy you something to eat, okay?"

"Aight."

Young and that bitch Tyesha been acting real funny tonight. "Ah Young, let me holla at you."

"In a minute. I see my sister over there. I'll be right back, my dude."

"Yo sister? Where?"

When his finger landed in the direction of where them Eastside Crazy bitches were standing, my dick got hard. I heard Tyesha say that she was going to the bathroom. I picked up my phone to call Big Moe. "Yo? I see those bitches right now. All of them."

"Handle them hoes, but you better not harm a hair on JoJo's head, Derrick."

"How you know---"

"Never mind all that. Don't miss this time."

CLICK!

I went to the bathroom, took off one of my t-shirts, and tied it around my face to hide my identity. When I came out, the lights were dimmed and the music was loud. *"Where the fuck are they,"* I said to myself.

I scanned the room for a few seconds before I spotted them over by the video games. BINGO! I walked around to the backside of the rink for a better shot. When I had it, I opened fire.

BOC! BOC! BOC! BOC!

I saw a few bodies drop as I turned around to run back to the restroom to hide my gun and put my shirt back on. As I rounded the corner, I ran dead smack into Tyesha.

"What the fuck? Why you got that gun, Lil Man?"

I knew I was gonna have to shoot that nosey bitch too. "Fuck you; slut ass bitch!" I raised my gun to her head.

"What the fuck are you doing? Get that gun outta my face. Meechie's gonna fuck you up!"

Why did she say that? "You can tell him that in hell, bitch!"

POW! POW!

I shot her once in the head and once in the mouth. "You talked too much, anyway."

After I got rid of my gun, I put my shirt on and ran outta the side door. I was laughing all the way to the bus stop. "Silly hoe! I got her and now I'mma get them tomorrow!"

Young Meech

"Miko, what's good sis?"

"What it do, lil bro?"

"Shit, chilling up here with my homie Lil Man, his girl, and Tyesha."

"Lil Man, who? Where you know him from?"

"We go to school together. Why? What's wrong?"

"Nothing, I was just wondering if it was the same Lil Man that we been looking for. Probably not. Anyway, you and Tyesha getting real close, huh?"

I had to smile because I was feeling shorty. "Yeah, I like her lil feisty ass."

"Where she go?"

"Ah, she went to the bathroom."

Just then, they hit the lights and turned on some banging ass music. "Shit, she need to hurry up. I'm tryna get my juke on."

Right after I said that, I swear I thought I heard a pop. I looked around and saw people scattering.

"AH SHIT! SIS, GET DOWN!"

"Fuck that! Let's go!"

"I gotta get Ty!" Whom the fuck would shoot up a skating rink full of kids? Fuck! Where is Lil Man? I know he got his banger on him. My heart broke into a million pieces as I saw young kids fall to the ground. Lives ending before they even began. "Miko, get outta here. I'mma find Ty and Lil Man."

"Hell naw! I'm strapped. Here! Find out who shooting!"

"Okay, get outta here! Meet me at Auntie Shawn's truck."

After a few seconds, the shooting stopped and the lights came back on. I heard screams from every direction. "OH MY BABY! NOOOO!"

Lil kids were stretched the fuck out everywhere.

"Young, we gotta go. The police is on the way."

I looked around to see if I saw Ty or Lil Man. Dirty grabbed me. "Come the fuck on! They probably already outside! We can't afford to get blamed for this shit!"

"You right."

JuJu

"Hurry up E, pull off!"

We all jumped in the car with the quickness. Whom the fuck shoots up a skating rink?

"Damn, did y'all see my cousin?" Each of them replied they hadn't. "Re, call Ty for me. My damn nerves are too bad right now."

"She not answering."

"FUCK! Where the fuck is she?" I'm in straight panic mode now.

Tiki put her hands on my arms and gently caressed me. "You know she's street smart. I'm sure that when she heard those shots, she got low too."

"You probably right. Y'all remember last year on the Fourth of July when I threw a M80 in the crowd, Tyesha was the first one to get ghost?"

Everybody started laughing. E was the first to speak. "I remember that shit. She was sitting next to when you threw it."

I hope she's good. "Well, y'all ready for tomorrow? Tiki, call Meechie and make sure we got the green light."

"I'm on the phone with him now."

"Put him on speaker."

"Aight, hold on."

"Hello?"

"Meechie, are you and ya boy gonna be ready tomorrow?"

"I just got off the phone with him. He said that he and Ty ran outta the side door and hopped in a cab."

"Thank you for that info. I was starting to lose my mind. See you in the A.M. WAIT! Have you spoken to her?"

"Naw, my homie said she mad because I didn't come for her. I'mma hit her up tomorrow."

"Okay, get some sleep. Be at the designated spot around 6 a.m."

"Aight, goodnight cha'll."

13 ~ Lil Mama

"**B**oo, get ready. I'm 'bout to come pick you up."

"Bitch, it's dark thirty in the morning. I ain't going nowhere."

"I'll be there in thirty minutes. Get the fuck up. We gotta go watch out for our babies today. You know they 'bout to turn shit up."

"Uggghhhhh! You get on my nerves. I'll be ready when you get here, bitch!

CLICK

I don't give two fucks about her being cranky. JuJu told me about that shootout at the rink. These ole senseless ass shootings. Some may think I'm wrong for supporting my niece's crime spree, but I say fuck whoever said that. They gon do what they wanna do anyway. It's up to me and Boo to make sure that they do it right.

I still had about thirty minutes before I left, so I decided to watch the 5 o'clock news and check the weather. As soon as I turned on the news, I shook my head.

"Reporting live from Channel Seven. We are following the shooting that occurred last night at the skating rink on 76th and Racine. Details are still sketchy. All we know is that three are confirmed dead. The two youngest that were found were twin boys found on the arcade floor. They have been identified as Donte and Dontell Sullivan. It was their eighth birthday. One body remains unidentified. If you have any information on this tragedy tonight, please, we urge you to come forward. Sharon Love reporting live. Back to you, Deborah."

"Damn that's fucked up. I grabbed my keys and headed out the door.

25 Minutes Later

I pulled up to where Boo was staying with a bad feeling in the pit of my stomach. One thing that I've learned from the FEDS and doing time for them is…Trust your gut.

I called JuJu instantly.

"Yeah auntie, what's up?"

"Y'all good?"

"We 'bout to head out now. Everyone's here except for Meechie's homie. He told Meechie he'd meet us at the spot."

"Don't say shit else about it. I'll be there. Don't even tell the rest of them. I don't even know the lil nigga and already I don't trust him."

"Me either. He told Meechie that he took Tyesha home in a cab after the shooting. She ain't answered her phone yet."

"Don't jump the gun. She might be asleep. I mean it is 5:45 in the morning."

"You right. Look, we 'bout to head out. I'll call you when we're done."

"I love you."

"I love you too baby. Be careful."

"Okay."

JuJu

I'mma kill Jaw's ole disrespectful ass. This bastard didn't even bother to come home last night. I got bigger shit on my mind, but as soon as we pull this off, I'mma punch that nigga in his eye.

"ReRe, did Poohman come home last night?"

She pulled on the blunt before passing it. "Nope and frankly I don't give a shit."

"Okay, let the games begin. Our target leaves her house every day at 6:30 a.m. We better head out so we can cut her off at the McDonald's."

"Aight E, you and Tiki be careful."

"We got this. We love y'all."

"We love y'all too."

Dirty E

"Why you smoking so much, Tiki? Are you nervous?"

"Naw, I'm just ready to handle this business."

"We good. This ain't shit for us. Meech got us, don't you kid?"

"Hell yeah. I'm alert and ready. This damn Red Bull got my ass ready to take off."

I looked down at my watch. "Come on, it's time to roll out. We got exactly ten minutes to catch the bank manager at Dunkin Donuts."

Lil Man

"I'm sure they said this bank, Big Moe. Damn, I do listen." This nigga gon make me shoot his ass.

"Make sure you call the police as soon as you see them go in the bank. I'm going to the other bank."

"Let me come with you."

"What the fuck did I say? Just do what I said!"

Big Moe (71st and Jeffery 6:30 a.m.)

I been waiting for my get back. I'm 'bout to get paid without even lifting a finger on these chumps.

Well, I'mma lift one finger…my trigger finger! Lil Man's info better be accurate. I'm 'bout to sit right here on 71st and Jeffery and see how this shit plays out.

Young Meech (79th and Stoney Island 6:37 a.m.)

"E, I'm already at the spot. I got a perfect view of the entrance."

"Aight, we already at Dunkin Donuts waiting for the bitch. We was going to go to the bitch's house, but this feels better."

"Alright, call me when y'all on the way."

Jaw and Poohman (71st and Jeffery 6:37 a.m.)

"Poohman, stop fucking laughing. This shit is serious."

"Man, calm yo scary ass down lil boy. I'm sure they did their homework on this place. I know the bank opens at 7:30. They should be long gone before then. We're just going to sit tight and watch their backs to make sure they get in and out safely. Pass me the blunt, nigga."

JuJu (6:50 a.m.)

Just as I was pulling up to the gas station on 76th and Stoney Island, the bank manager was going into the store. "ReRe, gone and go jump in the car with her."

"Bitch no! I'm 'bout to go in the store and get her."

Before I could protest, this damn fool was outta the car. This hoe is certified, I swear. As the lady was walking outta the store, Re was approaching her. I couldn't hear what was being said, but from the look on the manager's face, I could tell that she was scared as hell. The manager got into the driver seat, and Re got into the passenger seat. When they drove past me, this dumb bitch stuck her tongue out at me. "Dumb ass lil girl."

I looked at my watch and it was 6:57 a.m. We were right on schedule.

Lil Mama (71st and Jeffery 6:59 a.m.)

I sat patiently behind the driver's seat waiting for my niece to show up. The bank manager opens the door at 7:10 a.m. every day except for on the weekends. I'm ready for anything to pop off.

"Boo, have you heard from Jaw?"

"He told me the other day that he was on a mission. He just didn't say what. Why?"

"Just asking. You know how stupid those two get over Thelma and Louise."

I just so happen to cut my eye to the left and I almost died. "Oh shit! Girl, there them two fools go right there!"

ReRe (71st and Jeffery 7:03 a.m.)

"Park in the handicap spot in front of the entrance." I wanted to laugh. This lady was so scared that she was shaking.

"P-P-Please don't hurt me."

"Stop fucking talking to me and quit fucking farting. You been farting since we left the gas station."

"I'm sorry, b-b-but I'm nervous."

"Nervous my ass! You stink! QUIT!" This funky ass bitch was blowing me. I hit JuJu on the chirp. "Miss I'm that bitch, where you at?"

"Right behind you. Put yo face on."

"Let's go. Don't try nothing funny because I won't hesitate to shoot yo stanking ass."

LJ and Poohman (71st and Jeffery 7:05 a.m.)

"Jaw, look at them crazy ass broads."

All Poohman and I could do was watch our girls in action. "Poohman, I hope that things go as planned."

He looked at me and shook his head. "I know right, because I ain't physically ready for no damn gun battle."

"Mannnn, Poohman, I got chu my dude. I bought the big boy with me today." I reached under my seat and pulled out my TEC-9 with the extended clip. "Damn Poohman, they been in there for three minutes already. I'm getting nervous. Aww shit, Poohman look! Tell me that ain't that nigga Big Moe! FUCK! FUCK! FUCK!"

Young Meech (79th and Stoney Island 6:30 a.m.)

My adrenaline was pumping. I've never been on shit like this before. I'm ready though. I hit Dirty to see where they were. "Dirty, where y'all at?"

"I'm at the donut spot waiting for Tiki and the manager to pull up. We was supposed to snatch the bitch up here, but yo sister wanted to go play *Snatch a Hoe*. Man Meech, yo sister a beast."

I started cracking up because I could just imagine my big sis recking shit. "Well, come on. I been here for like twenty minutes. The police been riding through like every seven minutes."

Tiki (6:37 a.m.)

"Shut the fuck up, please. I said I wasn't gonna hurt you, but if you keep getting on my nerves, I'mma shoot yo ass."

This old ass lady been crying since I snatched her from her front door. "Mr. Know-It-All, head to the bank."

"Aight, hurry up."

This old bitch was driving as slow as hell. She was really testing me.

"You don't have to do this. You are such---"

WHACK!

I popped her ass on the side of her head with my pistol. "Save that shit. You better try and save your life and shut the hell up. Damn! What part of that…"

WHACK!

"Don't you…"

WHACK! WHACK!

"Understand?"

I saw that she was looking kinda woozy. "Bitch, don't crash this car."

Lil Man (79th and Stoney Island 6:50 a.m.)

Where the fuck are these bitches? I been here since 6 o'clock. I know I'm in the right spot. All I've been seeing was the police patrolling around this bank every few minutes. Who picks a bank on the corner of a busy intersection anyway?

BUZZ! BUZZ!

Damn! That's my phone.

"Hello?

"Don't forget what I said, Lil Man. Call the police as soon as you see them go in there."

This black bastard was starting to get on my nerves. "I'm not hard of hearing. I got you."

"I'm over here at the other bank posted up. As soon as I see them go in, I'm going to let them bat up all the money and then I'mma murk they lil asses."

Dirty E (79ᵗʰ and Stoney Island 6:57 a.m.)

I had to smoke a blunt to ease my mind. As soon as I put it to my lips, I saw Tiki pull right up to the front door. "Bout time."

When they got outta the car, I started cracking up. Tiki's silly ass was holding the old lady's hand as if she was helping her cross the street or something. As I made my way to the front door to catch up with them, I had this crazy ass feeling. "Maybe I do need to quit smoking weed."

Tiki looked back at me and winked her eye. "You ready?"

"Yeah."

She turned around and pushed the old lady towards the door. "Put the alarm code in, now!"

Lil Man (79th and Stoney Island 7:02 a.m.)

Here we go. I grabbed my phone and thought about it for a second. I wanted to kill them. I didn't want them in jail. "Fuck calling the police. I'm 'bout to shoot these hoes."

I jumped out the car and headed for the entrance to the bank. When I got to the door, I opened and closed it as quietly as possible. I heard noises, but I couldn't make out what was being said. It didn't matter. I pulled my gun out and walked to where I could see them. I wanted them to see my face before I got Pancho's revenge.

Dirty had her gun pointed at the old lady. "Hurry up and put the money in the bag."

Tiki walked over to the counter and filled another bag. I'mma take a bag or too for me.

"Mr. Know It All, are we gonna still do the thing?"

I didn't know what thing they were referring to, but I was about to do my thing.

"What up E?"

She had to do a double take. "What the fuck? Lil Man?" She looked down at my hand. "Oh so now you on some gangsta shit, huh?"

"Fuck you bitch! Y'all killed my brother! Now y'all can burn in hell with him!" I raised my gun at Dirty and pulled the hammer back. "Big Moe 'bout to kill them other two bitches too!"

Young Meech (79th and Stoney Island 6:57 a.m.)

Damn, I wish they would hurry the fuck up. I ain't sign up to sit in this car all damn morning. I put the blunt out for the third time, and when I did, I saw Dirty and my sister at the entrance of the bank with some old lady.

"Aww shit! Here we go!" I was so hyped that I was talking to myself. I perked up and got ready to do whatever was needed for them to make it outta there safely. A few minutes had passed and they were still in there.

"Hurry up y'all." At that moment, I felt in my heart that something wasn't right. As soon as I reached for the door handle, I saw Lil Man creeping in the bank. "What the fuck?"

I knew that nigga was cruddy. I watched him slither in the bank like the snake he was. I was so upset that I pounded my hand into the steering wheel. "I'mma kill that motherfucker!"

I waited for him to disappear inside the bank before I made my move. I opened the door to the bank and crept inside trying not to make a sound. I heard talking so I stopped to listen. "Oh so now you on some gangsta shit, huh?" "Fuck you bitch! Y'all killed my brother! Now y'all can burn in hell with him!"

This nigga done lost his mind. I can't believe I been chilling with the enemy all this time. "Damn!" I can't let this shit end like this for Dirty and my sister. I heard a gun cock, so I knew it was now or never. "Big Moe 'bout to kill them other two bitches too!"

Lil Mama (71st and Jeffery 7:05 a.m.)

"Oh shit Boo! Get up bitch, look!" I shook my friend outta her sleep.

"Bitch what?"

"It's Big Moe! NO! NO! NO! He just went in there after our babies!" I'm on the verge of having a panic attack.

Boo jumps up and punches me in the arm. "Fuck! I told you I wasn't ready for another gun battle!"

"Fuck all that shit! Let's go!"

We jumped outta the car and made it to the door in a matter of seconds.

"Boo, I got you sis. Just watch my back."

She was about to say something when outta nowhere Jaw came running up to the door.

"Jaw, where the fuck did you just come from?"

"Come on Lil Mama, when it comes to mine, you know I don't miss a beat!"

I was happy to see his ass. I got my gun out and readied for war.

"Grab the door Jaw and pull it open slowly."

As soon as he did, we heard two shots.

POW! POW!

I screamed, "OH NO, JU!"

Big Moe (71st and Jeffery 7:05 a.m.)

Before I made my move, I called Lil Man to make sure he did what I told him to do. After watching them two lil bitches go in the bank, it was time to make my move. I'm murdering everyone inside and taking all of the money. Hell, I deserve it. I casually walked to the entrance of the bank and entered as quickly as possible. The inside was quite small so it wasn't hard to locate them lil bitches. I stood still for a few seconds trying to hear what they're saying.

"Jackpot bitch! They must have just restocked the vault. Look at all the neatly stacked hundreds and fifties."

That instantly made my dick hard. The talking continued.

"Hurry up and finish bagging this shit up. What are you doing? You tryna memorize my face so you can tell the police what I look like? Look all you want, bitch! You'll never get the chance!"

It got eerily quiet. I was about to show my face and do my thing when I heard the sound of two gunshots.

POW! POW!

I pulled my gun out and ran towards that back of the bank when I heard someone scream, "OH NO, JU!"

ReRe (71st and Jeffery 7:07 a.m.)

When we got in the bank, I noticed it was small as fuck. "Man, ain't no money in here."

Ju told the lady to unlock the steel door that I assumed was the vault. As soon as she did, I was geeked. "Jackpot bitch! ! They must have just restocked the vault. Look at all the neatly stacked hundreds and fifties."

I whispered in Ju's ear and told her to get all the tapes from the security office. I walked back over to where the bank manager was bagging up the money. Instead of concentrating on bagging up the money, that hoe was giving me the ugly face. "Hurry up and finish bagging this shit up. What are you doing? You tryna memorize my face so you can tell the police what I look like? Look all you want, bitch! You'll never get the chance!"

I pulled out my Glock 40 and shot the bitch twice in the head. Not even two seconds later, I heard a familiar voice scream, "OH NO, JU! Ju get them bags and let's go NOW!"

I grabbed the bags and made a run for the door when, BAM! I ran smack dead into this big black bastard. "Who the fuck---"

He grabbed me. "Shut up bitch! Remember me?"

Before I could respond, I heard footsteps behind him. The voice I heard next was music to my ears.

"Naw, bitch ass nigga, remember us?"

Lil Mama, Boo, and Jaw were standing there ready to kill something. He was outnumbered and from the looks of things, this was gonna finally be his last ride. I don't know where Ju went, but she came flying around the corner right into the nigga's arms.

"Let me go!"

He had this smirk on his face that told it all. "Get the fuck back before I blow this bitch's brains all over this place! GET THE FUCK BACK!"

The look on Jaw's face set the tone for our next move. He threw his hands in the air. "Man, Big Moe you got it. Don't shoot my girl, nigga, because if you do, you gon die with her."

I was standing there shaking my head because this shit was going all wrong. Call me crazy, but that nigga was not gonna punk us like that. If she died, then so would he and the rest of his bloodline!

I blurted out, "Ju, I'm sorry!"

She had this unreadable expression on her face. "It's cool. I love y'all."

He snatched her backwards. "Fuck all this sentimental shit! Grab them two bags over there and let's go! Now I'm about to slide out this back door with her. If I think that y'all 'bout to run after us, I'mma shoot this bitch. Do I make myself clear?"

I rarely show emotion, but that nigga had a gun to my bestie's head. God, if he pulls the trigger… please let her go without suffering. Deep down in my heart, I knew that she was about to die. He had every intention on shooting her as soon as he was outta our sights.

As they reached the back door, he laughed. "Well guys, it was fun. I'll see all y'all in hell."

He opened the back door with his back and walked out backwards with Ju in front of him. Smart move. None of us had a clean shot. As soon as the door closed, we heard,

BOC! BOC! BOC! BOC! BOC!

I couldn't take it anymore. I fell to my knees and screamed, "JUJU!"

Poohman (71st and Jeffery 7:07 a.m.)

After we saw Big Moe enter the bank, I knew that there were about to be a few murders. Jaw decided on a plan that I thought was crazy, but I didn't have much of a choice. I waited a few minutes after Jaw, Boo, and Lil Mama run into the bank before I drove the car around to where I thought the backdoor would be. I thought that it was a dumbass plan because there ain't no way in hell that nigga Big Moe was gonna come outta that backdoor.

I sat there with the dumbest look on my face. I should have went in there with them. My woman was in there too. "Fuck! What's taking them so long?"

I was about to follow my first mind and take my ass in the bank when I heard loud talking by the door that I was now standing in front of. I couldn't make out what was being said, but I pulled my pistol out just in case.

About ten seconds later, the back door flew open and I saw the back of this big ass nigga backing outta the door with someone in his arms. He was laughing and taunting my peoples, "I'll see all y'all in hell."

I took a closer look and that's when I noticed whom he had in his arms. It was a chance that I had to take. Big Moe was too busy taunting Jaw and the rest of them so he never paid any attention to the rest of his surroundings.

JuJu felt my presence because when she looked to her left and saw me standing off to the side of the building, she dropped all of her weight to the ground.

BOC! BOC! BOC! BOC! BOC!

I shot him three times in the back and twice in the head.

"Come on Ju, we gotta go!"

Shit, she jumped in the car so fast that you woulda thought that she came to pick me up. She hugged me tight as I pulled off. "Thank you Poohman!"

"Damn girl, you go make me crash. Let go."

I drove to the spot where we was all supposed to meet after the job was done. "Ju, call Jaw."

LJ

Standing there watching that nigga pointing a gun at my girls head set my heart on fire. I wanted to kill that nigga. I had to act accordingly because one wrong move would end in this fool shooting my girl. So when he said to back the fuck up, it was a no-brainer.

ReRe gave me the look of death. I ignored her crazy ass. She'd rather shoot it out. If we made it outta there, I was gonna tell Poohman to take her ass to see somebody. I told Poohman to wait at the back door hoping that he'd use that door to make his getaway.

So far, it was working to our advantage because he was backing up in that very direction. I locked eyes with my boo and I instantly felt her pain. I had to look away. My heartrate sped up as that motherfucker did exactly what I wanted him to do. It pissed me off that I wasn't gonna be the one to send his punk ass to dance with the devil.

"I'll see y'all in hell." I prayed that Poohman's hotheaded ass stayed put instead of getting impatient and trying to come up in here. No sooner than I saw the door close, I heard five gunshots.

ReRe lost it! "JUJU!"

I grabbed her. "She good ma! We gotta go! Grab some bags Auntie Boo."

She looked at me like, nigga please. "My bad. Lil Mama and Re, grab those bags. We gotta go!"

As I picked up the last bag, my phone rung. "Tell me she's good, bro."

"We good nigga! Meet us at the spot."

Young Meech

"Lil Man, what the fuck?" I walked towards him slowly with my gun pointed at him and my finger on the trigger. If he so much as farted, I was gonna make his ass dance. He had the nerve to actually smile at me. "What up Bro?"

"What up? What you on, Joe?"

Lil Man started giggling like a five year old. I knew right then that, that nigga had snapped mentally.

"Young, how nice of you to join us."

"Why the fuck do you have that gun pointed at my sister?" I guess he didn't like that question because his ass snapped.

"BECAUSE YOUR SISTER AND HER FRIENDS KILLED MY BROTHER! T-THEY KILLED MY BIG BROTHER!"

"Aight, calm down. We can talk about---"

"AIN'T SHIT TO TALK ABOUT! I missed at the restaurant, but I won't miss today!"

"What? The restaurant? You hoe ass nigga! You shot at us at Fred and Jack's?"

He started giggling again. "I wasn't trying to hit you, Young. I just wanted them. Y-you shot me, Young. I know you didn't mean it, though. You didn't know it was me. I forgive you, but I'm killing these bitches today!"

I knew that if I didn't do something right then, his crazy was going to kill us all. "Come on bro, let's grab that money that's on the floor and go someplace and talk this shit out. This ain't really the place. I looked at my sister who was slowly easing her gun from behind her. I shook my head no, but it was already too late because Lil Man saw her.

"Oh yeah? Bitch, let's get it then!"

What happened next sent me into a blind rage. Miko snatched her gun out and pointed it at Lil Man, but he was quicker. He shot her in the chest.

"MIKOOOO!

She went down like a ton of bricks. Dirty ran over to where she had fallen. I rushed Lil Man knocking him to the ground.

"I'MMA KILL YOU NIGGA FOR SHOOTING MY SISTER!"

The nigga was possessed with something that wasn't human because he flipped me with the quickness.

"Y-y-you wanna fight me? L-l-let's go then!" He snatched me off of the ground and threw me into the glass wall that separated the lobby from the main area. I bounced up real quick, though. I ain't no pussy by far. I started punching that nigga in his face as if I was trying to rearrange it. He took every punch like a champ.

"That's all you got, Young?"

Outta the corner of my eye, I saw Dirty creeping our way with a crowbar in her hand. I tried to move outta the way, but Lil Man's crazy ass grabbed me.

"Where you going, Young? The party just began."

He flipped me off of him and got on top. I was still swinging and connecting every punch.

"You w-w-wanna keep hitting me?"

At that point, that nigga snapped. He made this crazy ass sound. "AGGGHHH!"

The nigga started scratching my arms and my face as if he was a damn alley cat. "I'MMA KILL YOU!"

I was losing my strength. "Dirty, get this nigga off of me!" I stopped fighting. Shit at this point, all I wanted to do was cover my face up.

BOOM!

That nigga screamed out, "OUCHHH!"

Dirty kicked him so hard he went screaming through the air. The shit was like a scene outta a Tom and Jerry episode. The nigga hit the wall so hard it knocked him out.

"Come on Dirty. Grab that money. Let's get the fuck outta here."

I ran over to where my sister was laying. She looked as though she was barely breathing. "Come on sis, you got to get up."

Dirty came running back in the bank after putting the bags of money in the car. "Come on Young, pick that bitch up! She aight! She just got the wind knocked outta her! Look, she got a vest on."

She lifted up Miko's shirt and showed me the vest. "Let's go Young before that nigga wakes up."

I looked at Lil Man's unconscious body on the ground and I felt sorry for him. I felt so bad that I let him live. That would be my mistake!

14 ~ JuJu

That was by far the scariest job that we have ever done. I can't believe that nigga Big Moe had a gun to my head. Poohman came through big time. It was as if he read my mind before I could say anything.

"You ain't gotta thank me. Jaw woulda done the same thing for Re."

I turned towards the window to clear my mind. My ringing phone brought me back to reality. "Yes Auntie Tae?"

"I guess you think since you out on your own you can keep my under aged daughter out for days at a time."

"What the hell are you talking about? Ty not with me and ain't been with me since the night before last."

"Then where the fuck is she? She ain't been home since she took her lil hot ass skating."

"She did go home. It was a shooting at the rink and we all got split up. She jumped in a cab with a friend."

"That's some bullshit and you know it! Find my child and tell her that I'm fucking her up when she comes home!"

CLICK!

Poohman was looking at me as if I was crazy. "What?"

"So y'all wasn't gon tell us there was a shooting at the rink?"

Damn! He continues, "Just like y'all won't gon tell us that y'all was planning to rob two banks at the same time."

I was speechless. I had to come back with something. "You and Jaw make moves that don't include us. We ain't kids, Poohman. We---"

I'mma let Jaw handle you, but I'mma get yo girl. Today showed me that yeah y'all 'bout that life, but y'all bumping heads with some real killers. But back to your cousin. She missing?"

"My auntie said she ain't been home since the night before last. Actually last night. Meechie said that his friend took her home."

"Then call Meech."

Young Meech

I can't believe how that shit went down. My best friend was my enemy the whole time. Auntie Shawn felt that shit too. Damn. He shot my sister.

"Dirty, you sure she don't need to go to the hospital?"

She waved her hand in the air. "She cool. The bullet went through the vest a little. After a few butterfly stitches and some alcohol pads, she'll be good. Ain't that right, Tiki?"

"Man, kiss my ass! I'm in pain, nigga!"

Dirty started laughing. "At least you're alive, unlike that nigga back at the bank. Ain't that right, Meech?"

I shook my head. "Naw, I didn't shoot him."

She whipped her head in my direction. "NIGGA ARE YOU SERIOUS?"

"I felt bad for him." I tried to make her understand that I had some type of love for the nigga. "That's like my best---"

"Fuck all that shit! Best friend my ass! Do you know he ain't gon stop 'til he kill us? Tiki, what the fuck, man?"

"Calm down, Dirty. Lil bro, that lil boy is fucked up in the head. We are responsible for his brother's death. Friend or not, he's going to die by the hands of one of us. He shot me too. That lil bastard got to go, Meech."

My phone rang so I hit speaker since it was JuJu.

"Man, Ju you ain't gon believe what Lil Man did at the bank."

"I probably would since he lied about making sure Ty got home last night."

"WHAT? Come on Ju! Tell me, my shawty good!"

I heard her sniffle. "I can't because we don't know where she at."

Tiki grabbed my phone. "JuJu, that lil nigga shot me in my chest!"

"WHAT?"

"And dig this. It's the same Lil Man from the hood."

"Are you serious? Ah, that nigga done something to Ty. Meet us at the spot."

"Which spot?"

"Mine."

(Twenty Minutes Later)

We all made it safely to the spot. Everyone was sitting around the living room telling a piece of what had happened today. Lil Mama called all the hospitals, police stations, and juvenile detention centers. Nothing!

Boo looked at her and said, "Call the morgue."

Lil Mama snapped, "WHY THE FUCK WOULD I DO THAT? SHE AIN'T THERE!"

I grabbed my phone and called Lil Man's phone just to see if he would answer. "What up, Young?"

I was shocked. I had to look at the phone for a second. This nigga is truly certified. I put my finger to my mouth to shush everybody. I put him on speaker.

"Nigga, what the fuck is wrong with you?"

"Shit, I just wanna kill those hoes because they killed Pancho! You and I can still be cool. You like a brother to me."

"So, I'm supposed to sit around and let you kill my sister?"

"Basically. Either that or you can die too. I really like you, but I could care less if you live or die."

"Damn, you cold as hell! Let me ask you a question. Where is Tyesha?"

He started giggling. "S-s-she probably in hell by now! Fucking tease!"

I had to walk away because JuJu almost screamed out. Had it not been for Jaw's quick reflexes to cover her mouth, she would have.

"What you mean?"

"I shot that bitch at the rink last night after I shot at them hoes you was with. Fuck them hoes, Young! You wanna come through and play NBA Live?"

I just hung up. Damn! Not my lil ride or die. I walked back in the living room and all eyes were on me. I had to put my head down. "Umm, Lil Mama, I think that you should try the morgue."

JuJu lost it, "TYESHA! NOOOOO! GET OFF ME, JAW! I'MMA KILL THAT SON-OF-A-BITCH!"

There wasn't a dry eye in that bitch.

"Damn sis, I'm sorry---"

"It's cool lil bro, come here."

I felt like I couldn't breathe. My heart turned cold with every sob I heard throughout the room.

"The morgue said that they have an unidentified teenage female there. She has the tattoo that Tyesha has on her wrist."

She threw the phone at the wall so hard that it flew into several pieces. Then she fell to the floor and screamed, "TY! TY!"

I hope Lil Man knows that he just killed everybody in his family.

15 ~ Detective House

(71st and Jeffery)

"Officer Dixon, this is what you call a hot mess. From the looks of things, this was a planned robbery. No forced entry and no damn security cameras."

This fits the M.O. of that Indiana robbery. I'm not jumping to conclusions, but I'd bet my paycheck that it has the E.S.C. crew all over it.

"Boss, we got a bloody mess out back. Come take a look."

On the way to the back of the bank, I stopped to look at the dead bank manager's body. "Damn, they did her dirty. Whoever did this has some serious mental issues."

Officer Dixon came walking towards me looking as if she wanted me to break her ass off. I had to literally adjust my dick in my pants. She caught the whole move.

"You so nasty! Stop looking at me as if I'm a piece of Harold's Chicken! Anyway, you ain't gon believe who's laid out in the alley."

"Amuse me."

"Ramone aka Big Moe Harris."

"I'm lost."

"Ugh. Don't you do your homework?"

"Only on things that matter."

"Well genius, this matters. Let me refresh your memory. J.R. Harris? Donte aka Boogie Harris?"

"Aw shit! Dude from the Indiana bank and dude from that kick door over on Marquette."

"Bingo!"

"Fuck me sideways!"

"No thank you."

I had to smile at her quickness. "Not you love. If I ever get the chance, I would fuck you straight, from the back, on your---"

"I get the point creep. This shit is connected."

My radio chirped. "Boss, you gotta get over here."

"Where?"

"5th and 3rd bank on the corner of Stoney Island. It was a robbery over here at about the same time that bank on Jeffery was hit."

"No shit?"

"I guess they forgot the plan because the bank manager escaped."

"Holy shit! I'm on my way. Escort them to the police station. I'll be there shortly."

I looked at Dixon. "We got a witness!"

(Fifteen Minutes Later)

After taking a look at the Stoney Island robbery, I was ready to get to the witness. I glanced at Dixon and noticed that she was deep in thought.

"What's on your mind, sexy?"

She smiled and licked her lips. "My sister is doing some time in the FEDS and I'm worried about her. Ever since our Dad passed away, she has been, well, different."

"Just be there for her. That's all you can do. When she gets out, move her to the Chi."

She laughed. "Chicago ain't ready for Moe Betta!"

I was speechless. People and their damn nicknames. "Moe Betta?"

She rolled her eyes. "Moe Betta, breaking them hoes for they chedda."

Why did I even ask? When we arrived at the station, I went straight to the interrogating room. I saw an old white lady sitting in a chair looking petrified. She was being questioned by one of our rookies. That dumb motherfucker was questioning her as if she was the main suspect. "So you mean to tell me that you are the victim?"

"Yes sir, I am."

"I don't believe you.

"I'm an eighty-one year old woman, young man. I am the victim. Didn't your mother ever teach you how to speak to your elders? I have told you the truth. I'll be happy to explain this story to you just one more time. I was at home getting ready to go to Dunkin Donuts because you know I gotta have my caffeine fix. I made sure to lock up my home. There's some crazy people out there. I walked to my car and was about to stick my key in the door when all of a sudden, a person walked up behind me with a gun and told me to shut the fuck up and get in the car. Excuse my French, young man. After we got in the car, I was directed to drive to the bank. I even tried to talk some sense into that child. Do you know that little heifer hit me?"

"Is that why you have that bruise on the side of your face?"

"Yes sir. She hit me several times. If she didn't have that gun, I had the right mind to bend her over my knee and spank her little tail."

I saw that the rookie was getting impatient with the old lady.

"Get on with the story, will you?"

I gotta admit that the old bat was snappy.

"Don't use that tone with me! Y'all little motherfuckers are all so damn disrespectful! You're lucky that I'm saved. Don't raise your voice at me again, do you understand?"

The rookie was taken back by her aggressiveness. "Yes."

"Yes what?"

"Yes ma'am."

"Now, that's better. Where was I? Oh yes, after she hit me several times, we finally arrived at the bank. She looked at me and said that if I didn't wanna die, then I should do whatever she said, so I complied. Hell, that wasn't my money in the bank. When we entered the bank, another person joined us. I don't know if it was a he or a she. Looked like a boy, but sounded like a girl."

"What do you mean by that?"

"It sounded like a girl, but it definitely looked like a boy. Stop interrupting me. My mind is not that sharp anymore. You better shut up while I can still remember."

"Yes ma'am."

"After the second person entered the bank, I just knew I was in trouble. After opening up the vault for them, I crawled under the counter and kinda just prayed that they would forget about me. No more than five minutes later, a third person came into the bank. Now that person came in with the intentions on harming the other two. I'm almost certain that they called him Gucci Man. No, no, no wait. They called him Lil Man. Lil Man called one of them E. That Lil Man guy also said that they killed his brother and that Big Hoe was gonna kill them other two bitches. Wait, not Big Hoe, it was Big Moe."

"So, Lil Man was claiming that the two in the bank and two more people killed his brother?"

"Right, but that's not it. Somebody named Young came in the bank and tried to talk Lil Man out of killing his sister. That's when I heard a shot. Somebody screamed, Miko after that. I was still praying that they forgot about me. I was scared outta my damn mind."

"You're doing fine. Do you wanna take a break?"

"No because I'm almost finished. Two people started fighting. I didn't see who, so don't ask. Now, that's all I know."

"You did well. Are you sure you weren't involved?"

"Young man, don't make me put these palms on you."

16 ~ JuJu

Tyesha's funeral was so beautiful. Her casket was all white with twenty-four carat gold handles. She was dressed in an all-white Donna Karen two-piece. Her hair was cut into a short Halle Berry style and her makeup was light, but cute. As we pulled up to the funeral home, I had butterflies in my stomach.

"Dirty, I want her." I burst into tears at that moment. I'm sure my cries and sobs could be heard throughout the city.

"It's okay Ju, let that shit out."

"Ty was such a pretty girl. She didn't even get the chance to live her life. E, I'mma make that nigga feel my pain."

It was packed inside the funeral home. The preacher gave a very touching sermon. "We gotta save our babies. Protect them, love them, guide them, and show them the right path."

As the preacher touched the hearts of all that came, I scanned the room just to see who came to show some love and I'll be damned if I didn't see Lil Man dressed like a fucking woman in the last row.

"Dirty? Why is Lil Man dressed like a bitch sitting in the back?"

Dirty turned her head and looked to where I was pointing. "Ju, I don't see him."

I snapped. "So you don't see that raggedy bitch all the way in the back with that blonde and black wig on with that ugly ass red silk looking shirt?"

She looked again. "Damn that's crazy! The nerve of that nigga!"

I was boiling. "Dirty, I'mma kill that nigga's mother tonight!"

"Ju, you know that ain't your area of expertise. Let me make that move."

"I ain't no baby, nigga. He killed my fucking cousin!"

I was getting amped up because people started looking at us. Jaw had to calm me down.

"Calm down Love. Where is Tiki?"

I was about to hit her phone when I saw her walk through the doors with this fine ass tomboy looking chick. She was light skinned, with bowlegs, and a curly ponytail.

"Sorry I'm late Ju. I had to wait 'til my boo got off of work. Everyone this is Ashley."

I had to be nosey. "Where you work?"

"I work in the third precinct."

I almost fainted. "Oh, so you a cop?"

"Yep."

(After The Funeral)

The repass was at Auntie Tae's. Auntie Tae was so extra. At the gravesite, she fell out on the ground yelling. I wanted to kick her stanking ass in the grave with Ty.

Lil Mama and Boo sat off to the side. They hadn't said much all day.

"Auntie, Lil Mama, you good?"

"I'm aight, baby. Just got a lot of shit on my mind."

"You know Lil Man came to the funeral dressed like a woman?"

"Seriously?"

"Yup. I'mma hit that nigga where it hurts."

"That ain't the type of talk to have right now, okay?"

I walked away to find Jaw. He and Poohman didn't come to the burial because they had moves to make, but he promised to make it to the repass. When I looked out the window, I saw my Auntie Tae talking to some man. She was all smiles and shit. Just an hour ago, she wanted to die. Now she was smiling so hard, you would have thought the bitch was trying to audition for a Crest toothpaste commercial.

I walked back into the living room and found Lil Mama. "Come look at this shit. I mean stuff."

Lil Mama helped Boo get up and they came to see what I was talking about. Boo's eyes became as big as silver dollars. She must have squeezed Lil Mama's hand because my auntie screamed.

"OUCH! Bitch, why you squeeze my hand like that?"

"How Tae know him?"

"Shit, I don't know. She probably fucking him. Why?"

"That's who shot me!"

"WHAT?"

"I'mma kill yo sister if she told him where I stayed. Let's go!"

Lil Mama went to pull the car around back. As I watched Tae and the dude's actions, I could tell that this wasn't their first encounter.

"Damn, shit just got real."

Tiki

The funeral was lovely. I had to come to support my bestie and my lil bro. I really felt bad for him. I also knew that all hell was about to break loose on the streets of Chicago.

"Meech, fix your face." I handed him a tissue.

Towards the end of the service, I could have sworn that I heard giggling. "Damn, I really need to leave that weed alone."

Meechie must have heard it too because he jumped up and began looking back and forth like a maniac. "Miko, that nigga in here. I can hear him."

"Who are you talking about, lil bro?"

"That pussy ass Lil Man. That's his ass giggling. Dirty, don't you hear him?"

Dirty reached for Meechie and told him to walk outside with her. My girl Ashley was real quiet.

"Boo, what's wrong?"

"Nothing. I'm just watching the scenery."

I met Ashley at Ford City Mall. She was doing security for Sally's hair store. I was there getting some hair products for my customers. I thought she was the cutest thing ever. I could tell that she was into the lifestyle. Don't ask me how. We just kinda know these things. I had to try my hand.

"Umm, excuse me."

She looked up and down for a few seconds before she spoke. "What?"

"What? I'm speaking to you, that's what."

"Lil girl, how old are you?"

Damn, I hated to lie, but I wanted her and I knew that she was much older than I was. "I'm eighteen and I'm far from a little girl. Let me get your number so you can take me out."

She started cheesing from ear to ear. "You feisty as hell Ma. I like that. My name is Ashley. What's yours?"

"Tamiko, but you can call me Tiki."

That was all she wrote. We've been together ever since. Yeah, I know she's a cop. That shit don't bother me. I keep her as far from my business as possible. After the funeral, we went to the repass. Tae's ghetto ass ordered chicken and fries from Harold's Chicken. After she made a fool outta herself at the burial, I ain't seen another tear since.

JuJu was the hostess and I must say that my boo was holding up pretty well.

"Ju, tell Tae somebody wants her outside."

Ju walked to the window being nosey I guess. Next thing I saw was Ju flying to where Lil Mama and Boo were sitting. After about two seconds, I saw Lil Mama help Boo to the window. Whatever it was pissed Boo off because they left shortly after that. Now I wanna be nosey.

"Ju, come here."

"What's good?"

"Why Lil Mama and Boo fly up outta here like that?"

"I don't know because they were whispering, but I do know that it had something to do with that detective that Tae is out there talking to."

Ashley looked at me all funny and shit. "A detective? Is he still out there?"

"Yeah. Why?"

Ashley got up and walked to the window to take a peek. I was right on her heels. "Aww shit! That's my boss!"

She looked like she was straining her eyes to get a better look at something. Then it must have clicked. "That lady is our informant on a case we're working on."

My mouth hit the floor. "What case?"

She turned to look at me and shook her head.

"Damn, I'm slow." She grabbed my hand and said, "Let's go!"

Lil Man

(GIGGLING) Ever since that bank shit, I couldn't stop giggling. I been on this emotional rollercoaster. It's crazy. I wanted to go to Tyesha's funeral, but I knew it would be dangerous. Then it hit me. I can use a disguise. "What should I wear?"

I ran upstairs to my mother's room. She had a bunch of wigs and shit. After finding the right outfit, I was out the door.

Once I arrived at the church, I must say that I was impressed. People really did like that little dick tease. I found a seat all the way in the back. I sat next to a few hoes from the hood that I knew. I hope they don't recognize me.

One of the broads had the nerve to have a baby with her. I mean, really? Who brings a brat to a funeral? The baby had to be about two. He had this damn sucker in his hand and he kept hitting me with it.

"Hey little baby, stop. Okay?"

He just smiled at me as if what I was saying was funny. "Shut up punk."

I was shocked. Ole ghetto ass bitch probably taught him to say that shit.

"Excuse me. Please tell your baby to quit hitting me."

That lil bitch got smart with me as if I was in the wrong. "Is he hurting you? He just a baby, dang."

That little shit was fucking up my plans. I was here to watch the crew and I couldn't because I had to keep telling that lil badass baby to stop. I got something for his ass. When his mother turned back around to talk to her friend, I grabbed his arm and I bit the shit outta his lil ass.

"AAAWWWW."

I sat back and acted as if I was so into my own world.

"Damn, Quisha you shoulda left his ass at home. Shut him up."

"I know right. Shut up Queshawn!"

Towards the end of the funeral, I saw Dirty walk Young outside. "Poor baby. I'mma kill them motherfuckers sooner than later.

When the funeral was over, I went home. I needed some rest and I had to put my mother's ugly ass wig back before she came home.

I thought about Young. I missed my buddy. Let me call him. I dialed his number.

"Why the fuck are you calling me?"

"Because I miss you. Don't be mad, bro. Let's meet up so we can talk."

It was quiet for a few seconds. I crossed my fingers because I didn't want him to say no.

"Meet me out west at the Circle."

"What time, Young?"

"8:30 and don't be on no bullshit!"

"Young, I love you. I won't try to hurt you."

I jumped in the shower and was out the door in a flash. "Damn, I gotta steal a car."

Dirty E

"Look Meech, you go ahead and meet him. I'mma go holla at his mama."

"Let me whack that nigga, E!"

"Naw, not yet. The point is for him to feel the pain he put you and Ju through. Go ahead and be careful."

I knew that Ju wanted to kill his momma, but I'm the enforcer. I make those types of moves. Nobody makes my besties cry and get away with it. Killing his momma is the least I can do. My phone started ringing as I was making my way to the car.

"Hello?"

"Boo, where you at?"

"Out. I'mma be late. Start the movie without me."

"Naw, I'll wait for you."

"Did you call yo sister and tell her you wasn't coming home tonight? Don't lie!"

"Yes baby, she knows. Hurry up and get here."

"Aight."

I checked my watch. It was 8:48 p.m. "The bitch should be at home."

I parked my car a block away from Lil Man's crib. I ain't want them nosey ass neighbors to see my car. After jumping a few gates and running through the gangway, I was at the front door.

KNOCK! KNOCK!

"Who is it?"

KNOCK! KNOCK!

The door came flying open. "What?"

I smiled at her. "Are you sorry?"

"Sorry for what?"

I raised my gun to her chest. "Sorry for giving birth to a pussy ass nigga!"

BOC! BOC!

I didn't even stay to watch her body drop.

JoJo

When I moved in with my sister Mia, I knew that it was gonna be fun as shit. That shootout at the rink was kinda normal for me. It didn't bother me one bit. I even met a cutie before all of that shit jumped off. Lil Man was cool, but I don't do dusty.

My lil friend and I have been texting back and forth for a few days. Tonight we supposed to make it a Block Buster night. She had to make a run so I'm chilling at her spot waiting for her to come back.

RING! RING!

"Hello?"

"What up, JoJo? What you doing?"

"I'm chilling, what's up Lil Man?"

"Are we still on the same shit? You know the plan?"

I rolled my eyes. "If what you said is true and those hoes killed my brothers and my big cousin Big Moe then I'mma lay they asses down."

"Don't sleep on me. I was taught by the best."

"I'll call you later, Lil Man."

I hung up on his ass and went to find me something to eat in the kitchen. "What's good in this bitch?" I walked in the kitchen and turned on the light.

"Aw shit! You scared me!"

"Did I?"

I didn't like the way that bitch was looking at me.

"Yes you did. When you get here, Tiki? I didn't hear you come in."

"I just walked in. Wanna hit this?"

"Naw, I'm good."

I made me a bowl of cereal and went back in E's room. That bitch might be a problem.

Tiki

What Ashley told me, blew my mind. I ain't know we was on the radar like that. She said that there wasn't any clear pictures of us. That was why she was sent to talk to Tae. The meeting never happened because Tae said she wasn't meeting with nobody but Detective House.

"Damn, we in some shit."

I tried to call E, but she wasn't answering. "Answer the phone, bitch!"

I figured E was on some slick shit. I pulled up to the crib and parked. I saw E's light on in her room. "Who the fuck up there?"

I crept upstairs and attempted to unlock the front door. Dumbass left the door unlocked. I walked in with every intension on cursing a bitch out until I heard a conversation that I'm glad I heard. "I'm chilling, what's up Lil Man? If what you said is true and those hoes killed my brothers and my big cousin Big Moe then I'mma lay they asses down."

"Oh yeah, bitch?" I sat on the couch in the dark and finished smoking my Kush blunt. I can't wait to tell E. She gon whack this lil bitch! She went to turn the light on and almost shitted on herself.

"Aw shit! You scared me!"

I smiled. "Did I?"

"Yes you did. When you get here, Tiki? I didn't hear you come in."

"I just walked in. Wanna hit this?"

"Naw, I'm good."

I watched her make a bowl of Fruity Pebbles and walk back towards E's room. I kept calling E. No answer.

"I'mma stay put. Shit, now I'm hungry."

I went to make a bowl of cereal for myself. "Dirty bitch!" She drank the last of the milk. I called my other two besties and put them up on game. She fucked with the wrong ones.

Lil Mama

"Ah, lil boy? Put that shit in the basement. That's where you bag up. NOT UP HERE!"

Damn dummy. I'mma kill Boo's ass. This shit ain't my cup of tea. I got Jaw and Poohman moving that work. I ain't no damn babysitter. We just opened up shop over here in Englewood and I already see that I'mma shoot somebody. Young Meech been my little shadow. He got the game on lock in his mind. I'm just letting him do him.

"Ah Lil Mama? There's a black Denali pulling up out front."

"Meech, you expecting company?"

"No."

"Where my gun?" I walked to the front porch with Meech two steps behind me.

Two dudes hopped out the truck and walked up to the gate. "Can I help you gentleman?"

Without a warning, Young Meech pulled out his gun and cocked it. I put my hand on his arm. "Whoa killa."

"Naw, Lil Mama. Y'all niggas better back the fuck up."

I turned around to address these niggas. "What cha'll want?"

The driver spoke, "You gotta shut this spot down. This Big T's block."

"Big T?"

"You got twenty-four hours."

I had to laugh at these lil playschool gangstas. "Fuck y'all and Big T! How 'bout that? Move the fuck around before I let my young boy do you dirty."

"Aight, your funeral."

The politely got back into their truck and pulled off.

"Meech, call your Auntie Shawn and find out who Big T is. We about to have a problem."

I walked back into the trap and looked around at these lil young dumb ass niggas playing X-Box. "Turn that motherfucking game off. As a matter of fact..."

POP! POP!

I shot a hole in the game system and the T.V. "THIS IS A DRUG SPOT, NOT AN ARCADE!"

When I walked off, I heard one of them lil bastards say, "That bitch crazy."

I yelled back, "Yo momma!"

Lil Man

I sat at the park all night waiting for Young. I had feeling that he wasn't gon show. I wish he woulda doe. I missed my homie. Why couldn't he see that I was all he needed? Fuck his sister. I looked at my phone and saw that I had five missed calls. I didn't really feel like being bothered, but something in my gut told me to return the call.

"Hello?"

"Who is this?"

"DEEERRRICCCK, SOMEBODY SHOT MOMMA!"

Instantly I started shaking. "W-w-what chu mean? Don't say that, Bessie! Who? What? I'm on the way!"

Oh no! I hope this is all a sick joke. I'm going to kill whoever thought that this would be funny.

(Fifteen Minutes Later)

The street was blocked off so I jumped outta the car and took off running towards my house. I knew it wasn't a joke when I heard my little sister screaming. "MOMMY, NOOOO!"

"Let me through, please! I live here!"

145

17 ~ Auntie Boo

My recovery has been slow, but somewhat successful. I needed to be at my best when I went after that nigga A. I mean, damn. I was really about to go to war with the fucking police.

Lil Mama been running shit with Jaw and Poohman. I know that drugs ain't her type of thang, but hey, she's doing well under the circumstances.

Today I was supposed to meet up with my new connect, Shawn. Apparently, there has been a problem with the shipments coming in on time. I can't make that move by myself so I called my big sister. "You feel like taking me to physical therapy?

"I'll be there in twenty."

(Twenty Minutes Later)

"Heidi, why you come pick me up with that shit on?"

"Because I'm grown. You can go by yourself."

I just shook my head. This bitch got on five-inch stilettos and an all-white leather one piece. If I didn't have a nigga gunning for me, that woulda been cool. "Where yo sidekick, Lil Mama?"

"Tapping with yo son and Poohman."

"You should let me run a spot."

I just looked at her.

"What? I could run a spot."

"And if somebody tried to rob you, what would you do? You don't like guns."

"Girl, I got mace."

I just laughed because that lady was crazy. After physical therapy, we decided to take Cottage Grove all the way up to 75th because I didn't wanna take the expressway. We were sitting at the light on 35th when I looked to my left and saw a car coming at us fast as hell. "AWW SHIT, HEIDI DRIVE! IT'S A HIT!"

It was already too late.

BOOM!

This big ass Tahoe rammed the driver side door. I pulled out my Glock 40 and started bussing.

BOC! BOC! BOC! BOC! BOC!

I hit the passenger in the neck. "HEIDI DRIVE!"

She was moving her leg around, but we weren't moving. "BITCH, WHAT ARE YOU DOING? DRIVE!"

"I'm trying to kick these damn heels off, bitch! I can't drive under pressure in these damn shoes!"

Finally, she stomped on the gas and we took off. I almost shit on myself when I saw who was behind the wheel. "That's the fuck boy! DRIVE! DRIVE!"

We sped towards the police station on 35th and State.

"Boo, should I pull in the parking lot and make a run for the front door?"

"Hell naw! For one, I can't run, and for two, bitch he is the police! Hit the E-way!"

Heidi jumped on the expressway and burned ass.

"Boo, what the hell, girl?"

"I know sis that was crazy."

That mothefucker getting real bold. "I gotta call Lil Mama. If we don't get at that nigga, he ain't gon stop 'til he kill us."

"US?"

I looked at her scary ass. "Yes us, bitch. He knows who you are, dummy! No witnesses!"

"Damn Boo. I can't even be cute around you. I gotta put my war gear on."

"War gear? I know you not talking 'bout a scarf, white t-shirt, and some jogging pants?"

"Don't forget the Vaseline. What's wrong with that?"

"Ummm, how about everything! You coming to fight. Bitch, they shooting at us!

Lil Man

The officer wanted to be a dickhead. "Young man, I'm going to have to ask you to back up and let us do our jobs."

"B-b-but my momma is in there."

Something inside of me snapped. I found the strength that I didn't even know I had.

BOOM!

I pushed officer dickhead flat on his ass and ran to the front door where everyone was gathered.

"M-MOMMY? UGGGHHH! NO! NO! NO! NO! NO!"

I fell to my knees and bawled like a baby. Two officers came and tried to remove me from the premises. "Let me go!

POW! I punched the first officer square in the eye.

"Dammit John! Grab that little shit!"

"Come here kid! That's assault on a---"

POW!

I punched his ass too. "Fuck y'all!"

I ran back to the car and pulled off. I started giggling. "Somebody is going to die!"

18 ~ LJ

(The Plan)

The New Year was just two months away and it was time to make a couple of moves. JuJu doesn't know it, but come January First we're leaving the city. Poohman agreed to take Re and do the same thing.

It's about to be a bloodbath around this bitch. Motherfuckers tried to kill my Auntie Boo and my Mom Dukes. I can't have that. The plan is for Boo to rock that nigga to sleep, Me and Poohman are going after Tank, and Dirty is gonna handle Lil Man's ass. Simple!

JuJu

"So you mean to tell me that she's Big Moe's cousin?"

Tiki looked me square in the eyes and shook her head yes. "I know what I heard."

"Well, did you tell Dirty yet?"

"Nope. I was wondering what we could do to eliminate that situation."

"Well after I kill Lil Man's mother---"

"Bitch, you slow. E already killed that lady."

Baby, when I tell you that shit pissed me off. OHHH WEE! "That's some bogus ass shit! I had that! How E---"

"Girl bye. All of a sudden, you wanna be a killer? Miss me with all that. You know E is 'bout that life. Not saying that you not, it's just that she's the enforcer."

I could only sit there shaking my leg and roll my eyes.

"Come on Ju, we loved Ty too. When you hurt, we all hurt."

"I know Tiki. I just wanted to shoot that bitch."

"Okay gangsta. You was probably gonna knock on her door and when she opened it, you was gon turn your gun sideways. Let me find out you was gonna tell that hoe, "Break yo' self fool".

We both started cracking up.

"ReRe said she was gonna take care of JoJo."

I looked at Tiki as if she was nuts. "No ma'am. Let E take care of that shit. On another note, what are we doing for Thanksgiving?"

"I don't even know. Maybe yo Auntie Lil Mama could deep fry a turkey or something."

My mind was all over the place. It was about to be a bloody mess around this bitch. I just hoped that we came out on top as we did the last time. "Tiki, what's good wit ya police hoe?"

"Shit, once she gets all the information that they got on us, she gon let me know."

"Don't be pillow talking wit that hoe. She is still the police."

"I got chu. She on my side anyway."

"Tiki, I don't care. Let's go ride down on Jaw and Poohman. I'm tryna be nosey."

"Ju, we are so out of it. How much did y'all get from that bank job?"

"I didn't tell you? Oh girl, my bad. We got away with $76,581."

"That's it? E and I got $90,510."

"Tiki, we need to stick to robbing the white folk's bank."

"Yo ass stupid. Let's go!"

Young Meech

After talking to my Auntie Shawn, I was on fire. It had been a few years since I had heard that nigga's name. Big T turned out to be Tank. The same Tank that was responsible for my father's murder. Lil Mama was staring at me so hard that I had to tell her.

"What's on your mind Young boy?"

"The nigga Big T is Tank."

"Oookkayyy, who is that?"

"The nigga who had my father killed."

"Aww shit! What chu wanna do youngin?"

"I'm ready to get at that nigga."

"Well, you know that I gotcha back. Call Jaw and Poohman and tell them to come through. We might need the extra fire power in case those niggas come back."

(Thirty Minutes Later)

Jaw, Poohman, JuJu, ReRe, and my Auntie Shawn were all in position. "Call that nigga, Auntie Shawn."

"I already did. He's on his way."

Just as I was about to walk into the house, three black Denali's pulled up. I jumped off of the porch. "Come on Lil Mama; let's go see what's good with that nigga."

She looked at me and had the nerve to laugh. "Sit cha lil ass down. Come on Shawn. Jaw? Get ready to shoot if they get to acting stupid."

I was offended. "I'm still coming. Ain't no bitch in me. This 'bout to be my city."

My auntie shook her head, yeah. We all walked outta the front yard up to the curb. The doors of a Denali flew open and Tank jumped out. "What up Lashawnda?"

"Terrance?"

I was mugging the shit outta ole boy. He looked at me and smiled. He stuck his hand out towards the car and a smaller hand grabbed his. What I saw next sealed the deal. Tank was a dead man.

"Hello Demetrius. Are you gonna just stand there? Come here and give yo momma a hug."

Auntie Boo

"Hello, may I speak to Detective House?"

"Hold on one second. May I have your name?"

"Just tell him, Marie."

I knew that this was it for me. I couldn't live my life knowing that this bastard was gunning for me. I gave Jaw and Lil Mama the connect that they needed to take over the streets. JuJu and her little go-getters had the robbery shit on lock. My job was done. If I was going to hell, then I was taking that crooked motherfucker with me.

"He said you can just go on back there."

"Thank you ma'am."

My heart was racing. I couldn't turn back now. I walked to the door that had his name on it in big gold letters. "How the fuck did a snitch get to become a badge toting police? Crooked ass city, and fucked up ass justice department."

I opened the door and smiled. "I hope you said your prayers this morning, detective."

He blew me a kiss. "Devils don't pray, bitch!"

What was I doing? I didn't come to talk. I pulled out my Desert Eagle and let his ass have it.

BOC! BOC! BOC! BOC! BOC!

He fell to the ground. I was so in awe about what I had just done that I never saw the officers rushing to his aide.

The first two bullets that hit me knocked me down. "Put that gun down, motherfucker!" I spun around on my knees and the bullet that was fired to my heart was the one that ended it all.

"BOO! BOO! WAKE THE FUCK UP, BITCH! Quit all that damn screaming! Shit, you scared the shit outta me!"

When I woke up, I was drenched in sweat. "Girl, that dream was too real. We better hurry up and find that nigga."

I got up and went to take a shower. JuJu told me that Tiki's lil girlfriend is his partner. I got an idea.

"Heidi?"

"What psycho?"

"We gon have to find a way to get him away from the precinct."

"Umm genius, how we gon do that?"

"I dunno. Let me make a few calls."

I will say this thought. Come the New Year, Chicago will be a distant memory. I got up off of the couch and grabbed my car keys. "Come on, Heidi."

"Where too?"

"I gotta go see Pete."

"Girl, now you know that man ain't finna, let me nowhere near his place of business."

"Let's go!"

I called Pete on the ride over.. I had a feeling that I was being hunted. It was time to turn the tables on that nigga.

"Hellllo? Boo, where the hell you just go?"

"Far away from this place. Where my phone? I gotta call Pete. Hello? Hey Pete, I need you."

"Well, I like the sound of that. You know I've always wanted you. Damn, Boo you're so sexy---"

"Wait. What? I don't need you like that, fool. Pewww!"

"I knew that. I was just playing. How can I assist you?"

"Open the damn door. I'm outside. Umm, I got Heidi with me."

"N-n-noo! That bitch c-can't come b-b-back in here! That bitch is a big ass b-bully!"

I started laughing so hard that I had tears coming outta my eyes. "Why the fuck are you stuttering?"

"B-b-because that big bitch tra-traum-traumatized me!"

Heidi must have had enough. "Oh, I got cha big bitch. Open this gahdamn door before I kick it off of the hinges, you pussy!"

I just shook my head as we got outta the car. When we walked in the door, Pete's ass took off behind the bulletproof window. I was too through.

"Cut that scared shit out and come over here. Heidi ain't thinking about yo ass."

He slowly unlocked the door and came to where we were seated.

"I need an address for Detective Aaron House."

19 ~ JuJu

(Two Weeks Later)

Thanksgiving was two days away and everyone had been doing a good job with pitching in. My Auntie Lil Mama was having a small dinner party at her place. It was definitely time to turn up!

Jaw and Poohman's spots were really doing big things. We didn't have to hit a bank for a while. Today I was supposed to meet up with Tiki and her boo thang to see what was going on with the investigation.

"Jaw, why you over there looking all ugly and shit? I gotta go holla at Tiki. Wanna joyride?"

He just looked at me with a look of pure disgust. "Who the fuck is Slim?"

"Huh?"

Aww shit! It was a boy from school. I had accepted his friend request on Facebook. We just flirt back and forth. Harmless shit. Think bitch, think!

"It's a friend from school. Why you all in my shit, anyway? I don't say shit about yo phone ringing off the hook all hours of the night, and before you try to say some bullshit, all them calls ain't from crackheads."

"Delete his ass as your friend!"

"I don't tell you what the fuck---"

Before I could finish my sentence, he was all in my grill like a damn maniac. "Do what the fuck I said!"

Don't you know how when you and ya boo get to beefing and you wanna keep arguing just to piss him off more? Well from the look on his face, this was definitely NOT one of those times.

"Okay Jaw."

"Didn't you say we was going to Tiki's? Let's go then."

Tiki

"Baby, we're having company. Get dressed."

I ain't been doing much of shit lately. I been laid up with my boo. On some real shit, I been running my mouth to her ass so I been watching her like a hawk. If she farts and it smells like deceit, I'm murdering her ass.

"Tiki let me ask you a question."

I hate when people start off like that when they wanna know something.

"Go head."

"Why you lie about your age?"

BUSTED! "Huh?"

"You heard me, girl. You know I could go to jail for fucking with yo lil young ass. Not to mention, I'd lose my job and have to register as a fucking sex offender."

I would ask how she found out, but really?

"Well first off, I didn't know you. I really ain't got no excuse. I knew that you was older so I stretched the truth a lil bit. I fell for you Ash."

She shook her head and smiled. "I fell for you too, but we gotta slow down. I like you a lot, but I'm not going to jail for fucking with ya young ass. We can still kick it, but I'm not fucking you 'til you turn eighteen."

"WHAT? I mean---"

I couldn't get the rest of my words out because Ju and Jaw came walking through the door.

"Bestie, what you all loud for?"

I looked at Ashley. "We gon finish this later."

I walked in the living room to greet my girl and her boo. "Sit down! You not gon believe who the informant is that's telling the detective things about us."

JuJu looked at me with this worried expression on her face. "Try me."

"Yo funky ass Auntie Tae!"

Jaw had to put his head down on that one.

"Be for real Tiki, why would she do that?"

"Because for some reason, she wants all of y'all dead."

We all turned around to see Ashley walking into the room with an envelope in her hand. "Anybody familiar with the name Pancho? No? Well, apparently your aunt was fucking him."

"I ain't never see him at her crib."

"Well, from what she told my boss, they were dating. I could lose my job for all this, but I gotta warn y'all. He's coming for you."

JuJu got up and began pacing. "Why the fuck is he coming for us? We ain't got shit of his."

She looked at me and I put my head down.

"Tiki? NO!"

"She's my woman. You can trust her."

"YOU STUPID ASS BITCH! SHE'S THE POLICE!"

"Oh, I got cha bitch, JuJu! You can't whoop me!"

"Now I know you been smoking too much weed, Tiki. You know I'll drop yo ass."

This shit was about to get outta control.

"We ain't about to fight JuJu so calm down."

Jaw got up off the couch and grabbed Ju's arm. "Let's go. Call her later."

She just looked at me and shook her head as she walked outta the door.

"Jaw, I didn't---"

"I know Tiki. Let her cool off. I'mma hit yo phone later."

When he closed the door, I took a deep breath. I hope I didn't make a mistake by trusting Ashley's ass. If that hoe crossed me, then I was going to have fun killing her.

"Tiki, don't stress it. Let her calm down. She'll be okay."

"I know. Damn man. Tomorrow we're supposed to have dinner at Lil Mama's for the holidays."

"Well, let's hope that she's calmed down by then."

Dirty E

After all of the shit that we've been going through, I'm really looking forward to chilling at Lil Mama's for the holidays. I'll be glad when this year is over with. Bye Chicago.

"Hello?"

"Dirty, do you know that my Auntie Tae is the one giving the police information on us?"

"WHAT?"

"Yes and that ain't even the half of it. Why is that old *Drunk in Love Bitch*, Tiki over there telling her police girlfriend that we had something to do with Pancho's death?"

"NO THAT HOE DIDN'T!"

"E, yes she did! I was so mad I wanted to punch her ass!"

"Ain't gon be no punching! We don't fight! I don't give a fuck how wrong she is, Ju!"

"But E---"

"But E, my ass! We're family!"

"After the dinner, we are all going out to handle everything and everybody that ain't right."

"So you know about JoJo then?"

"My girl JoJo? What about her?"

"Well, call Tiki's big ass mouth since she likes to run her mouth. See you tomorrow."

CLICK!

No that lil girl didn't hang up on me. I had a feeling that something wasn't right with shorty. I just thought she was young minded.

"Ah, Tiki? What's good with JoJo?"

"OHHH Ju ain't shit! Baby, you might wanna sit down."

ReRe

I'm always down around the holidays. My mother' dead and my sick ass father is still in prison for her murder. If I didn't have my besties, and now Poohman, I'd lose my mind. I love em' so much. Cross them and you're as good as dead. I just got off the phone with Tiki. After the dinner tomorrow, I'm going to kill Tae.

I hate that I have to take someone from my besties, but if I don't, she's going to take all of us down with her. We are taking over the city. We don't have room for errors. My phone brought me outta my thoughts.

"Hello? Tiki? What?"

"Change of plans. After the dinner tomorrow, go kill JoJo."

"E's not gon be mad, is she?"

"Who cares? Girl, I told her what ole girl was on and that fool said that she was going to holler at her about it after dinner tomorrow."

"Tiki, I think that E should handle her own situation."

"What the fuck ever! If she hurt E, all hell is going to break loose."

I hung up on Tiki's ass. I don't have a problem laying a bitch down, but I'm sure that E is going to handle that.

"Poohman, you feel like riding to the store with me? I gotta get some shit for dinner tomorrow."

"You want Big Daddy to ride with you?"

"I got yo Big Daddy, aight."

20 ~ Lil Mama

I've been up all night cooking. I'm tired as hell. I've already knocked out the collard greens and turkey necks. My chitterlings are almost done. Let me call Boo's ass so she can bring that drank.

"Boo? Stop at the Kenwood Liquor Store and grab me some Patron."

"Don't get to acting stupid off of that damn Tequila because if you do, I'm fighting yo ass tonight."

"Aww girl, whatever! I'mma behave. You know we got big things to do tonight."

"I know sis. You ready?"

"Hell yeah. Pete gave me the low down on a few things."

"Good! Let's just come together and enjoy tonight."

"Sounds like a plan. On some real shit, that sounds so scary coming from your mouth like that. It kinda sounds like *The Last Supper* type shit."

"It might be!"

Boo

"After we eat and enjoy a few drinks, we going to get that nigga, Heidi."

"I just want us to be okay."

"We will. I gotta kill him, sis. If I don't, he gon keep coming for me. Plus, he got the city on lock. We fighting the law. I got everything that we gon need. Pistols, bulletproof vests, night vision goggles, and some more shit. Come on here. Let's go hit Kenwood."

"Now you speaking my damn language. I need a drink bad as hell for tonight. My nerves are bad."

I grabbed my keys and was about to head outta the door when something told me to turn around. Heidi was coming outta the back bedroom. This bitch makes me sick. She had on some neon pink stretch pants with the matching zip up hoodie.

"I told you to wear something low key and unnoticeable."

She looked herself up and down. "What? Bitch, I'm comfortable."

"Heidi, we about to go kill somebody and you standing here looking like a neon glow stick. GO CHANGE!"

JuJu

"Baby, why you so quiet?"

He just looked at me. I walked over to him and sat on his lap. "I'm listening?"

"After the party is over, Me, Lil Mama, Poohman, and Young are going after Tank."

"Can I tell you something?"

"Yeah."

"Me, Tiki, and Re are going after Tae."

"Hell naw Ju! Let Lil Mama handle that!"

"Lil Mama?"

"Yeah, that's her sister. Grimy or not, she loves her."

"It's done! She's the one telling on us. Lil Mama's going to understand. Shit, she told on her too."

I got up and grabbed the stuff that I was taking to my aunt's house. "You ready to go?"

"Hell yeah, I'm hungry."

Young Meech

"Auntie Shawn, are you still coming?"

"Yeah baby, I just got a few things to handle before I leave. I'll meet you there."

Tonight was the night that I was going to finally get my revenge on that hoe ass nigga Tank, and my scandalous ass mother.

"Meechie?"

"Huh?"

"No matter what, don't pull the trigger on yo mother. I know you don't care if she dies. Just make sure it's not by the hands of you."

"Okay Auntie. Why you ain't coming?"

"Because it's your time to do you. You ready nephew. I'm just here to back you up. The streets are starving for a new king. I see yo daddy all in you. Go out there and take over them streets. I'll meet you at Lil Mama's. I love you!"

"I love you too!"

Dirty E

After finding out that JoJo is Big Moe's cousin, I've been dying to kill that hoe. Ole disrespectful ass hoe. Thought she was gonna get the drop on me and my besties? I got something for that hoe for sure. It's a shame because she got some good ass pussy.

"JoJo? You almost finished? We need to hit the gas station. I need some blunts."

"I'm coming, boo."

I went through her phone last night and found out that she has been in touch with Lil Man. I could only imagine what the fuck they have been talking about. I've been sleeping with my gun under my pillow. Good thing she doesn't move a lot in her sleep. I woulda been shot her snake ass.

"After dinner, I got us a room with a Jacuzzi."

"Aww shit! You on some freaky shit, boo?"

More like killing yo ass type shit. "You could say that. Come on, I'm hungry."

Tiki

"Ash, grab my shirt outta the closet."

"Which one?"

"The all-black one."

I'm ready to laydown that bitch Tae. I never liked her anyway. How could she try to get at us like that? We broke bread with her funky ass. Greedy ass bitch!

"Tiki, my boss just texted me. He said after dinner to come see him. So after I eat I'mma burn out, okay?"

"Okay, that's cool. After we eat, me and the girls got a few moves to make anyway."

"Like what?"

"Here we go. Stop being the police all the damn time. You my woman too, or did you forget?"

"I'm your woman by default, remember?"

"Aww girl, fuck you. Let's go!"

ReRe

I never get nervous when it's time for me to kill somebody. Especially when they deserve it. Tae should have known better. Sorry for her.

"Come here, Re."

"What's good, love?"

"Be careful tonight."

This nigga is always in my business. Nosey ass!

"What---"

"Don't insult my intelligence, boo. I know the look."

I just smiled. "Maybe you do. You be careful too. If you come back hurt, I'mma murder everybody that you were with."

He stepped back and looked at me. "You serious?"

"As a heart attack. Come on, I'm hungry."

Lil Man

From what JoJo told me, everybody will be at Lil Mama's for dinner tonight. That's even better. This will be a Thanksgiving they'll never forget.

Some of y'all may think that I'm the bad guy, but I'm not. My life has been a struggle since birth.

I loved my mother to death, but she was a sick ass woman. I was a product of incest. My brother

Pancho was also my father. My momma was molesting him for years. I guess that once he got old enough to produce sperm, I was created. That's some sick ass shit, huh?

My sister TuTu knew. That's why they always fought. When I was born, Tutu babied me. Pancho did too. He always told me that I was the best little brother in the whole world. I think I turned out okay.

I sometimes tend to burst out in a fit of giggles, but other than that, I think I am fine. I just want revenge for Pancho and I intend to get it.

"JoJo, when you get this message, call me. I'mma start at Shawn's crib and then work my way down. Tae is next on my list. I'll try to make it to the party. Save me a plate."

21 ~Auntie Shawn

Damn, I'mma be late as hell. I'm hungry too.

RING! RING!

"Where the hell is my phone? Hello? Helllooo?"

Here we go with all that prank calling bullshit. Let me call Meechie's lil ass and let him know I'm on my way before he lose his mind.

"Nephew? I'm walking outta the door right now."

"Okay, we all over here. Hurry up!"

"I am. I--- Shit! The power just went out. Did you leave that damn fan plugged in again?"

"No."

"I'm on the way."

I hung up the phone and tried to make my way through the kitchen to the drawer so I could get my flashlight.

BAM!

"SHIT!"

I hit my damn shin on the damn coffee table. I grabbed the light and headed for the basement. As I made my way down the stairs, I could have sworn that I heard somebody giggling.

"Who the fuck is in here?"

No answer. I heard the giggling again.

"Who the fuck is playing with me?"

I moved the flashlight back and forth. I didn't see shit. I found the breaker box and tried to find the main power switch.

"Hi Shawn."

I looked. "Lil Man? What the fuck are you doing in my basement?"

"Um, I came to give you a message for Young."

"So you had to turn my lights off to do it? Lil boy if you don't turn my lights back on, I'mma kick yo ass. Turn them back on NOW!"

This crazy lil shit started to giggle again. Something ain't right and I need to get the fuck outta this basement with him. My gun was upstairs on the kitchen counter. Shit!

"Turn these lights back on and meet me upstairs."

I turned to walk away. Sadly, that was the mistake that cost me my life.

"On your way to hell, could you tell my mommy I miss her." He raised his gun and...

BOOM!

"Aghhh!" I dropped to my knees.

"Why? I took care of you."

"Bitch please. You never liked me anyway. Just die."

BOOM! BOOM!

"Two to the head, and now this bitch is dead!"

Lil Mama

"I'm glad that everyone is here. Y'all lucky I felt like cooking."

Everyone laughed. Looking around the table, I felt so much love. In a matter of months, we've managed to take over the streets. It's not what we did; it's how we did it...low key! My niece and her friends got that ski mask shit on lock. Jaw and Poohman's team are able to do what they are doing because for one, they are not greedy. They share the wealth.

Taking over doesn't necessarily mean that you have to rule everything. As long as you and your team is eating right and living well, life is great. We bow down to NO ONE! Any threats will be properly disposed of. Tonight we're taking out the trash.

"Okay, shut the fuck up so I can pray. My stomach is touching my back."

I looked at Meechie. "Where the hell is Shawn?"

"I dunno. I been calling her. Start, she'll be here. Ain't no way she 'bout to pass up some good ass food. Who's praying?"

"My house, my prayer. Bow your heads. Father God, I pray to you asking that you bless us all in a very special way. Touch all of us, Father God. Protect us from the enemies that surround us. Forgive us for our sins. Let us enjoy this dinner and each other's company. Protect us as we attempt to eliminate our enemies. God be with us. Amen!"

"Damn, Lil Mama this food good as shit. Will you marry me?"

"Shut up Jaw!"

Boo

"Joke time. Lil Mama? Remember when we was in Danbury and you beat the shit outta that ugly ass girl, Carey?"

"Here we go."

JuJu was the first to speak. "Who was Carey?"

"This old Dwyane Wade-looking ass bitch that was tryna fuck with my girlfriend."

All the kids screamed, "GIRLFRIEND?"

"Yes girlfriend. I had a lil piece in there."

Boo smiled. "Remember when you whooped Swag's ass in the hallway?"

"You play too much."

Now it was Heidi's turn to clown. "Who the fuck is a Swag?"

Lil Mama just rolled her eyes. "Boo, fuck you bitch. Don't get too drunk hoe. We got moves to make."

After about another two hours of joking and laughing, it was time to get shit cracking.

"Heidi and Lil Mama? Come here."

We walked to Lil Mama's room and finalized our plans.

"Me and Heidi 'bout to go see that nigga A."

"Where he live?"

"On 67th and South Shore Drive. I gotta go see Pete before we go over there. Pete supposed to have a key card for the downstairs door. Don't ask. What's the deal with that nigga Tank?"

"Him and his bitch are holed up in an apartment in Englewood, bitch. All that money and he wanna stay in the hood."

"I guess he feels protected over there. Boo, there's a gang of GD's over there. Shit, we gotta move on him like *now*."

I shook my head. "Damn, you ain't got Lucky's number?"

"Yeah, he gon make sure we get in the crib. He can't stand Tank. He said the nigga ain't letting them eat over there."

"See, what'd I just tell you? Can't be greedy. The hood'll turn on you."

I looked at Lil Mama. "Don't let Meechie kill his momma."

"I told Shawn, I got that. I'mma rock that hoe to sleep. Don't worry."

I hugged her. "Be careful, lil sis."

Heidi rolled her eyes. "Boo, let's go. She gon be aight."

Lil Mama gave her a look. All I could do was put my head down.

"Heidi, you'sa jealous ass bitch."

"How about this jealous bitch fuck you up?"

"I'm not even 'bout to play with yo big ass."

Lil Mama pulled out her 22. "I'mma pop yo ass in the kneecap, bitch."

"What you think my son gon do?"

"What you think my niece gon do?"

I had enough. "Aight. Y'all sounding like some fucking five year olds right now. Shut up and let's go!"

22 ~ JuJu

"Auntie Lil Mama, let me holla at you before we break out."

We dipped off to the side so that we could have some privacy.

"What's up lil girl?"

"You know that I'm 'bout---"

"I already know baby. Are you sure you can handle that?"

"I know I can.

"Then go send that bitch to meet her maker. When I found the time, I was gon eventually blow her brains out. I just didn't want to hurt you because I knew that you had some type of love for her grimy ass. Maybe this will ease your mind. She's not really your auntie."

"What?"

"She was your mother's best friend. Our mother took her in because her family didn't want her treacherous ass. I'mma tell you something else and you better not say shit to nobody. You already know that she was the reason that I went to jail? Well, I was going to kill her before I went to jail because I found out that she was the reason your mother disappeared."

"Oh yeah?"

"Apparently her and your mom went to a party at Bungalow Beach. There were drinks flowing, music playing, and people having a good time. At the end of the night, your momma walked to the pier to look at the boats. Well, she never came back, and to this day, her body has never been found."

I almost broke down. Here I thought that my mom ran off and left me. That's what Tae told me.

"Don't cry JuJu. Go get that bitch. Be careful and be safe."

She hugged me and walked away. Jaw saw the look on my face and came to see if I was okay. "What's wrong, boo?"

"I'mma kill that bitch!"

Dirty E

"Come on shorty. Let's make a move."

"Okay. I'm full as shit. Let me go use the restroom first."

I thought to myself, *"You better had enjoyed the meal since this yo last one, hoe"*

"Code four. Let me holla at y'all. Y'all know I'm 'bout to kill that bitch, right?"

Tiki was the first to speak. "Bout time nigga."

"Man shut up. Anyway, after y'all handle that issue, come get me."

Ju was looking as if she wanted to say something. "Speak chick."

"Why the hell do we have to come get you? You got a car."

Tiki laughed. "You better have a Plan B, dummy. So let me get this shit straight. After you whack her ass, you gon sit in the room and wait for us to come get you? You'sa sick bastard!"

"Fuck you, hoe. Meet me at the crib when y'all finish. Come on JoJo. Say goodbye."

"Bye y'all."

Boo

On the ride over to Pete's, I didn't feel right. "Heidi, call Pete."

She picked up her phone and dialed his number. "He ain't picking up."

When we pulled up to the lot where his building sat, I felt as if I was going to throw up. "Don't pull in the parking lot. Park in the front by the fire hydrant."

We got outta the car with extra caution.

"Pete?"

Nothing. I walked around the counter and almost passed out. "DAMN!"

Heidi came walking behind me fast. "Damn, what? Aww, hell naw!"

Poor Pete was lying face down in a pool of blood.

"Now Boo, who the fuck would do that to him?"

"Somebody that didn't want him sniffing around in their business. Let's go, we got a body to drop."

The ride to A's apartment was quiet. I knew that Heidi was thinking about that shit with Pete. I know it got to her. "You don't have to do this, sis."

She glanced at me. "Bitch, we in this shit together. Naw, I ain't no killa, but don't push me."

We both started cracking up. "Aight, 2-Pac. Pull over right there."

We parked and got out. We walked to the trunk and got out the things that we needed.

"Heidi, put this on." I handed her a vest.

"This motherfucker too little."

"That little motherfucker will save your damn life!"

After we geared up, it was show time.

"We not taking the elevator. The stairs are to the right."

Heidi stopped. "Well, what floor does he live on?"

"The tenth."

"TENTH? Now you asking for too much."

"Shut up and come on, girl."

The lobby was empty.

"Boo, ain't there supposed to be a front desk man or somebody to greet us?"

"This ain't the damn Hilton."

She was right though. It was already too late to turn back. When we finally reached the tenth floor, I told Heidi to pull her gun out and follow me. "Apartment 1003."

We checked every door until we stood in front of the right one. "Boo, why is the door cracked open?"

I was about to say something when the door flew open. There stood me and A, face to face. He had a smile on his face that told it all. We were fucked!

"Come on in, killa!"

I turned just in time to see this big ass nigga creeping up behind Heidi.

"Heidi, watch---"

He snatched her up like a ragdoll and dragged her into the apartment. "Let me go, motherfucker! I ain't that type of girl!"

A smiled at me and said, "Your turn."

I walked backwards thinking of a plan when I felt a presence behind me. "Walk forward or die!" I felt that cold steel being pressed to my spine. FUCK!

A pulled me by my hair and slung me into the apartment. "OUCH! STUPID MOTHERFUCKER!"

He closed the door "No my dear, you are the stupid one for coming here. You were trying to carry out a terrible attempt on my life."

"You shot me."

"So."

"You're a snitch!"

Heidi shook her head. "How could you? Ole bitch ass nigga. You better hide behind that badge."

He looked like he wanted to fuck her up. "Man, Bear? Shoot that bitch."

He attempted to raise his gun towards her. Big mistake!

WHAM!

Heidi hit him so hard that you heard his jaw crack throughout the apartment. A started laughing. "Damn, I shoulda warned him."

Heidi turned our way to say something when he fired, hitting her in her chest.

POP! POP!

"HEIDI?"

I ran to check on my sister. I checked for blood when I almost fainted. One of the bullets went through the vest. "Baby, hold on. I'mma get us some help."

He walked towards me still holding his gun. "Shoulda had a better plan, bitch!"

"I'll see you in hell, pussy!" I hocked up a big ass glob of snot and spit it dead in his face. He raised his gun and I knew that this was it.

"You won't see me in hell bitch, because I'm untouchable!"

POP! POP!

Lil Mama (66th and Ada)

"Jaw, you and Poohman go through the alley and wait for my call. Come with me Young."

I got ready to walk off when Jaw spoke up. "Hell naw! No offense, but Meechie ain't gon be able to protect you. He's too little."

"Little? My nigga, you must not know. My guns bust. Ain't shit little about me, but my tolerance for bullshit."

I just smiled. Shawn is right. He is ready. "Okay boys, we're not about to have a pissing contest. What do you think Poohman?"

I knew that he would side with Jaw. "We stick together."

"Aight, let me call my inside man. Hello?"

"Yeah shorty, go ahead and get ready. T and his bitch upstairs. There's two niggas in the living room and he got two big ass dogs that sleep outside of his bedroom door."

"Aight, he gave me the low down. Basically shoot everything moving. He's got two big ass dogs guarding his room. Please shoot them. I fucking hate dogs. Any questions? No? Let's do this!"

As soon as we hit the porch, I saw the curtains move. "GET DOWN!"

TAT! TAT! TAT! TAT!

BOC! BOC! BOC!

All you heard was guns blazing everywhere.

"Jaw, kick the door open."

BOOM!

The door flew open with ease. Cheap ass niggas can't even get a good door? The dogs came running at us with the intentions on eating us the fuck alive.

"SHOOT THEM DAMN DOGS!"

POP! POP! POP! POP!

Damn, Meech's aim was dead on point. I had to look back at Jaw and shake my head.

"Meech, stay close to me!"

We quickly swept the crib as if we were the FEDS. Surprisingly, we found Tank and his bitch trying to get dressed...dummies! If I heard all that shooting, I woulda run up outta that bitch asshole-naked.

I had to ask him. "Tank, how the fuck do you got all that money and you wanna lay yo head in the hood? Englewood at that?"

He looked at me as if I was shit under his shoes. "Who the fuck are you?"

Meech stepped up. "Don't worry about who she is. You need to worry about who you took from me."

It was as if a light clicked on in his head. He turned to his woman and slapped the shit outta her. "Didn't I tell you to take care of that lil nigga?"

"Demetrius, get the fuck over here! What the hell is wrong with you?"

Meech looked at her with a sideways glance that made me shiver. "Bitch, you gon die with him!"

I tried to stop him. "MEECH, NOOOOO!"

He raised his gun at her head and emptied the clip.

BOC! BOC! BOC! BOC! BOC!

Tank almost shit his pants. "L-look her Young Blood, you can have it all. The city, the money, the dope, everything. Just let me blow town."

"Did my father beg for his life?"

He was doing too much talking for my liking. Just as I was about to move towards him, I saw the chrome pistol Tank had underneath his pillow. "MEECH, SHOOT HIM!"

CLICK! CLICK!

Dammit! He was outta bullets!

"I see you outta bullets, Young Blood."

Poohman came from the shadows. "I'm not though!"

BOC! BOC! BOC!

Nothing but face shots.

"Come on, let's go! The dope and money are at the safe crib in Dolton, Illinois."

JuJu (88th and Marquette)

I was floored by what my Auntie Lil Mama told me. Tae was indeed a foul ass bitch.

"ReRe, you and Tiki wait out here and make sure nobody is being nosey."

She rolled her eyes at me. "You know better, lil gangsta. We are all going in and coming out…TOGETHER!"

"Aight."

I reached in my pocket and pulled out my door key. I opened the door as quietly as possible. The T.V. was on and a cigarette was burning in the ashtray. Tae was nowhere to be found. I looked back at my besties. "Y'all hear that?"

I heard a bumping noise upstairs. I whispered, "Upstairs."

We all crept upstairs like true assassins. I pointed to Tae's room. The bumping noise got louder and louder. "What the fuck?"

I pushed open the door and what I saw made me throw up my damn Thanksgiving food. Lil Man was on top of Tae fucking her in the ass. She was dead!

He looked up at us with sweat beads pouring down his face. "H-hey Ju. You wanna be next? I'm almost finished."

"Eeeew ReRe, shoot him!"

He stopped humping her and jumped up. He had blood all over him. He started giggling. "Shoot me?"

I barely blinked and he was flying through the air coming at us screaming, "ARGGGHH! I'MMA KILL Y'ALL!"

I jumped outta the way just in time. He hit the wall hard as hell.

BOOM!

That shit didn't faze him. He bounced right back up.

"RUN!"

We practically jumped down the stairs. We had guns, but we were seriously trying to put some distance between his crazy ass and us. When we got to the bottom of the stairs, Tiki was the first to fire.

POP! POP! POP!

One hit its mark.

"OUCCHHH BITCH!"

He rolled down the stairs holding his arm. I was outta breath. "I dropped my gun!"

Re looked at me. "Me too!"

That didn't stop her though. She ran over to the stairs and commenced whooping his ass. "I'mma kill this faggot with my bare hands!"

Tiki and I were right behind her. Two minutes later, and everyone out of breath, we stopped.

"Re, is he dead?"

She stomped on his head again. "He better be."

I had seen enough. "Tiki, go grab our guns so we can get the fuck up outta here."

Tiki ran back upstairs and grabbed our guns. She hit the stairs two at a time. I was glad that Tae was dead. ReRe just shook her head. We turned around at the same time to see Tiki walking down the stairs. Once she got to the bottom, she tried to step over Lil

Man. That was the mistake that cost my bestie her life.

He jumped up outta the blue and stabbed her in her throat.

"TIKI!"

She dropped the guns to grab her throat. At the same time, Lil Man reached down picking up one of the guns and shot her in her head at point blank range. BOOM!

I lost it! "NOOOOO TIKI! PLEASE NOOO! TIKI!"

ReRe snatched me by my arm and we took off outta the front door. Not even four steps outta the door, we heard three more shots.

POP! POP! POP!

"RERE NOOOOO!"

I dropped to the ground. "Wait Re, we gotta go back for her!"

"NO JUJU! SHE'S GONE!"

We ran to the car and jumped in. I was hysterical! "TIKI!"

Re drove away from the scene with tears streaming down her face. "Damn Tiki," was all she said.

Dirty E

"Yeah bitch! Aww shit, right there! Suck my strap, bitch!"

I was putting that lil hoe to work before I blew her brains out. "Turn around. Arch yo back."

After that, I rammed my ten-inch strap in her pussy full force. I was trying to split her ass in half.

"E-E-E t-t-that hurts, but please don't stop!"

I knew that hoe was a freak. "Yeah, take that!"

Earlier when we first got to the room, I slipped her a date rape drug. I put it in her drink. She shoulda been on her way out. I kept pounding away.

"E, I'm sleepy. Stop boo."

I slowed my pace down and after about two more minutes, she was out like a light. Let me call they asses to see where they at before I shoot this hoe, I thought. I hit JuJu's phone.

"E, SHE'S GONE!"

That was all I heard. I couldn't understand anything else, she said. "Stop screaming and tell me what's wrong! Who's gone?"

She kept hollering in my ear so I hung up on her ass. I called Re's phone. She picked up, but all I could still hear was JuJu's ass screaming. "What's wrong, Re?"

She was too calm. That shit scared me. "Lil Man just killed Tiki."

"WHAT?"

I instantly threw up all over the hotel rug. "Re, please tell me that ain't true! Not my baby! Please tell me something different! PLEASEEE!"

"I can't. Meet me a JuJu's crib."

CLICK!

I just stood there looking at that hoe lying on the bed sleep. "Lucky bitch!"

I punched her in the back of the head and got dressed. I shoulda killed that bitch!

Boo

I just knew I was a dead bitch. I closed my eyes after hearing the two shots.

"I never expected to see yo ass, but bitch thank you!"

"I knew he had something up his sleeves when he texted me and said that we were going to take a dip in Lake Michigan. I told Tiki I would make sure that y'all was good."

Tiki's lil girlfriend came through, big time. "Let's go before we all go down for these bodies."

She looked at me and said, "Bodies? It's only him."

I walked over to Bear and shot him in the forehead. "Now it's two. He was gonna shoot my sister."

I looked at Heidi and smiled. "Get yo ass up. You got grazed."

She was holding her chest. "Bitch, I'mma thug now. I got shot too! I'm getting a tattoo over this hole!"

I smacked my lips.

"Bitch, there's barely a scratch."

"You are a hater, Boo."

23 ~ Young Meech

After we hit the safe spot, I was numb. I just killed my mother. Crazy as it may sound, I feel no way in particular. "Fuck that bitch!"

Lil Mama looked at me and frowned. "Huh? Fuck who?"

"I was just thinking out loud."

We took so much dope from that nigga's spot that it was ridiculous.

"My Auntie 'bout to be so happy because we killed that nigga. As a matter of fact, take the dope to her crib. She got a raw ass stash spot in the basement."

Ten minutes later, I was pulling up into her garage. "Jaw, help me take the dope down to the basement."

"Come on, lil killa."

Lil Mama's phone rang before I could ask her to help us. She got outta the car and walked off.

"My Auntie Shawn still here. Come on. She's probably downstairs."

Lil Mama

The streets of Chicago are about to have a whole bunch of problems outta that Young Meech. I let him handle his business as he saw fit. I just didn't want him to shoot his mama. I promised Shawn that I would handle that. I hope she won't be mad when she finds out.

"Fuck that bitch!"

"Huh? Fuck who?"

"I was just thinking out loud."

I zoned back off into my little world. I hoped that everyone did what they were supposed to do tonight. Eliminate all the threats.

I pulled up into Shawn's driveway and parked behind her car in the garage. Meechie was asking Jaw to help him put that shit up when my phone rang. I stepped out the car and walked away so that I could have some privacy.

"Hey niecy pooh. Are y'all okay?"

All I could hear were sobs.

"Aww shit! Baby, what's wrong?"

"Lil Man killed Tiki."

I dropped to my knees. "OH GOD, NO!"

I started bawling like a baby. Poohman jumped outta the car and ran to me. "What the fuck? Get up!"

I just couldn't. That lil girl was like a daughter to me. Poohman literally snatched me off of the ground and held me. "What the fuck is wrong?"

I had to get it together. Who the fuck wanted to tell somebody that just killed their own mother that his only sister just got killed? I know I don't!

"Poohman, Lil Man just killed Tiki."

"WHAT? OH MY---"

He didn't even get to finish his statement. We heard a scream that was so painful it would haunt my heart forever.

Jaw

"Ah, where the light at in this bitch?"

"Shit, I tried to flick em. The fuse must have blown. Grab that flashlight and come on."

I was on Meechie's heels. It was pitch-black walking down the stairs. "Where's the box?"

He pointed to the left side of the basement. I started to walk, but I almost slipped on something thick and sticky.

"Meech, why is it wet in here my nigga?"

"Shit, who knows. My auntie be having all types of shit going on. There go the box."

I grabbed the flashlight from him and pointed it to the floor. "Man Joe, this ain't no water. Y'all got pets?"

"Hell naw."

I flipped the switch to the fuse and all the lights came on. There was blood everywhere. I looked to the right and saw a body under the stairs. I pulled my gun out. Meechie was just coming from another room when all hell broke loose.

"Jaw, I don't know where my---"

He paused and looked at what I was looking at. He walked to where the body was lying. His chest started to heave up and down for a few seconds before he collapsed. He fell onto the body and let out a scream that chilled the blood in my veins.

"UGGGHHHHH SHAWNNN!"

I ain't gon front. That shit broke me down. I walked to him and wrapped my arms around him. He held her tight and I held him tighter. I couldn't say shit. I heard footsteps coming from upstairs so I jumped up and pointed my gun at the top of the stairs ready for whatever.

Poohman and Lil Mama came flying down the stairs. Lil Mama stopped dead in her tracks. "Oh no, Shawn!"

She turned around and broke down in Poohman's arms. Shit, even Poohman started crying. Poohman shook his head back and forth. "We gotta call the police."

I thought about it and I told Lil Mama to stay with Meech. "Poohman, help me get all that shit up outta the safe."

I walked him to the safe and both of our mouths fell open. "Damn Jaw, she was holding."

Poohman gave me an eerie ass look that made my stomach flip. "What nigga?"

"Lil Man just killed Tiki."

My heart broke into pieces. "Where the fuck---"

"They cool. This city is about to turn into a warzone. Fuck Iraq. We 'bout to rename this bitch, CHI-raq! Meech 'bout to go on a murdering spree until he finds that nigga!"

"Who's about to tell him?"

"Shit, I hope Lil Mama does it."

After we moved all the work, we called the police. They asked us a bunch of questions. Most of them were bullshit, really. Everybody from State to the Lake knew who she was and who her brother was. Lil Mama called the team and told them to come to her crib.

On the ride to her spot, Meech was quiet as hell. I didn't have it in me to say shit to him because once he found out about Tiki, I was probably gon have to shoot his ass. How much could a person take before they snapped mentally? We were all about to find out.

Lil Mama

Everybody sat in my living room in silence. Boo, Heidi, and Ashley hadn't made it there yet. When JuJu and the others got there, though Tiki wasn't with them, Meechie automatically knew. He walked over to JuJu and hugged her tight. They both cried like babies.

"Did she suffer?"

Sensing that she was about to lie, he warned her. "Don't lie!"

She put her head down and cried. "Yeah, he did her wrong."

They sat down and you could hear a rat piss on cotton because it was so quiet.

A car door slammed. I looked out the window and saw Heidi, Boo, and Ashley coming up the stairs.

"Bitch, you hit that nigga so hard, I heard his jaw crack."

They were all smiles until they saw the looks on our faces. Boo quickly scanned the room and when her eyes landed on the girls, she broke down. Ashley did the same thing, and as if a bulb popped on in her head, she snapped.

"FUCK! FUCK! FUCK! NOT MY LIL MAMA!"

That bitch lost it! I thought she was gonna pull her gun out. I looked at Heidi and she must have sensed what I was thinking because she got into "Knock a Hoe Out" mode.

I walked up to Ashley and held her. She finally broke down and cried.

"Who did this to her?"

"We don't know," I lied.

She was Tiki's girl, but we were her family. Revenge will be ours. Believe that!

24 ~ Detective Malone

"Are you fucking serious?"

"Yeah boss. House and Blake are dead."

"Where the fuck is House's partner? Find her and tell her I said to get her ass in my office, NOW!"

The mayor is going to have my ass for this one. SHIT! I wondered what the fuck went down. I told that stupid ass nigga to stop with the extra shit. I put him in charge because he had the balls to get shit done. I've been knowing that kid since he was a little street punk. He assisted the FEDS with a few cases back in the day. He did such a good job that I spoke with some of my supervisors about him. They agreed to send him away to a police academy in a different state. I thought it be best if he stayed away for a while. You know, let the city forget his face.

When I felt the time was right, I brought him to my precinct, showed him the ropes, and ultimately put him on to my side cash schemes. I was too far up in the ranks to be out there shaking down drug dealers.

A was perfect. He was young, ambitious, and violent. I knew that he had a few things that he wanted to settle once he returned. I told him to do that shit on his own time. He fucked up when he shot that bitch because she didn't die. I wonder if she's behind this.

"Wendy?'

"Yes sir?"

"Get a tail on Marie Georgette. She lives at 8415 Marquette. She might know what happened to Office House. I want her followed closely."

"10-4. Boss, we got a call from crime stoppers that I think you might wanna follow up on."

"Fuck no, I'm busy."

"It's about that double over on 88th and Marquette."

"No shit?"

KNOCK! KNOCK!

"Come in."

"You wanted to see me, sir?"

"Yes, Officer Dixon, have a seat."

25 ~ Lil Man

I got revenge for my mommy and some for Pancho. Three more to go bro! Killing Tae was a bonus. I knew that she wasn't shit anyway. She was never good enough for Pancho. I hate a snake bitch! When Pancho stopped showing me attention and affection, I knew that I was gonna eventually kill her ass.

I really didn't want to kill Tiki, yet. I just got one outta the way. Better for me. I wanted JuJu, but fuck it. I'mma get them all. I'mma need some help. Who can I call? I thought about it for a second. "JoJo!"

I hoped that her dumbass wasn't dead. I warned her that Dirty was likely on to her by now. Let me call that hoe. "Where you at?"

"Come get me, Derrick."

"What's wrong? Where you at?"

"At the Camelot on 91st and Cottage Grove."

When I got there, she was leaning up against a wall, barely standing. She threw up when she got in the car.

"Bitch, you was just outside. What the fuck?"

"Fuck you! I don't feel good. I think E tried to kill me. I think she slipped something in my drink, but when I woke up, she was gone. I wonder why she didn't kill me."

I started giggling. "She left because I'm sure her besties called her and told her that I killed Tiki."

"You killed Tiki? Good! That hoe made me nervous. I think she heard a conversation we had a few days ago."

I rode around for hours. I knew that we were going to need some help. I was going after the rest of them bitches.

"JoJo, we gon need some help. Where all yo ghetto ass cousins from the projects at?"

"I'll round them up. We just need to lay low because they're coming for us."

"Let em come. I'mma BOSS!"

"Derrick, shut the fuck up. I know it's about to be a bloody mess around this place. We gotta stick together."

I looked at her and licked my lips. I rubbed her leg. "You know I'mma protect you."

SMACK!

She slapped my hand off of her lap. "Let's get one thing straight. This pussy if off limits. Don't try me like that!"

I laughed to mask my anger. Fuck her. I'mma kill them and then I'mma kill that bald headed ass bitch!

JuJu

Today was the day that we were going to lay my bestie to rest. We made sure she went out in style. Her coffin was pearl white with twenty-four carat gold handles. She was dressed in an all-white linen dress. It was simple, but she looked like an angel.

I couldn't believe that this was the last day that I was going to see her face again. Jaw came into the room and gave me the tightest hug. "Come on Ja'ziya."

"My government, huh? I'm good. You ready, Jaw?"

He hugged me again. This time I broke down. "I can't believe that she's gone! What the fuck? It hurts so badly. I'mma kill that bastard."

"Man, chill out love. Let's send baby girl home in a peaceful way. We'll deal with that other shit later."

The funeral was packed. There wasn't a dry eye in the house. The whole Eastside of Chicago was in attendance. I turned to the left and there was Tiki's mother walking down the aisle with some random ass nigga that I ain't never seen before. She stopped at the bench we were all sitting on.

"I should have took her outta this neighborhood a long time ago. Y'all ain't nothing, but a bunch of hoodrats and hoodlums."

Before I could say anything, Lil Mama jumped up. "Bitch, you better move the fuck around before yo ass get beat the fuck up in here. The nerve of you to speak to my niece like that. Who the fuck you calling a hoodrat? Don't you have AIDS? Yeah bitch, you do. You ain't even know your daughter. She wasn't no hoe like you. You better go on before I put your ass out."

She rolled her eyes and started talking shit as if my auntie was a joke. "I can see where you got---"

WHACK!

I barely had time to get out of the way before my auntie smacked fire out of her ass. "You will not disrespect your daughter's funeral. A funeral that I'm paying for. Jaw? Show this bitch to the curb!"

Jaw did as he was told with Meechie close on his heels. She had to make a scene on her way out screaming.

"GO STRAIGHT TO HELL BITCHES!"

I put my head down. That was so uncalled for. The last view for her body was the worse. E broke down. "NO, NOT MY DAWG! TIKI, I'MMA KILL THAT MOTHERFUCKER!"

Boo had to take her outta there. I was dreading the burial. We followed the pallbearers out to the hearse and I almost shit on myself when I saw what was waiting on us. There were like ten police cars out there.

"What the fuck?"

I looked through the crowd for my Auntie Lil Mama. As usual, she got ghost on our ass. Boo came up and held my hand tight. "Walk. They looking for you."

I almost fainted. "WHAT?"

"Shut the fuck up---"

Three officers came up to us. "Ja'ziya Campbell?"

"Yes?"

"Come with us, please. You are under arrest for the brutal murders of Shauntae Morgan and Tamiko St. Clair."

The last thing I remembered before I fainted was Boo screaming. "DON'T FUCKING TOUCH HER!"

Lil Man

Giggling. I couldn't chance going to Tiki's funeral. That was a no-no. I had another plan in mind. I called crime stoppers and told them that I had information on the double murder on Marquette. They said I could remain anonymous. JoJo and I sat across the street from the funeral home and just watched.

"I hope they give her ass life."

I looked at her and smiled. "Why?"

"Because that's one less hoe we gotta worry about."

"Who's next?"

Lil Mama

When I saw all of the police cars, I politely got the fuck outta dodge. I had my gun on me. How was I going to explain that to my parole officer?

Boo has been blowing my phone up. "Ma'am, I can't talk and drive dirty."

"Well, pull the fuck over. The police just came and took JuJu."

"Took her, for what?"

"They said that she was under arrest for the murders of Shauntae Morgan and Tamiko St. Clair."

Oh my goodness! Murders? How was I going to get her ass outta this shit?

"Boo, I'm 'bout to bust a U-turn and come get you."

I veered to the left and pressed on my brakes. "What the fuck?"

"What's wrong, Lil Mama?"

"Bitch, something wrong with my brakes. I can't stop!"

I was so wrapped up in trying to figure out what was wrong with my brakes that I never saw the semi-truck coming at me.

HORN HONKING!
By the time I looked up, it was too late.
"OH GOD, BOO!
BOOM!

MY BESTIES, THE DOWNFALL
Coming Soon!

Books by Good2Go Authors

Good 2 Go Films Presents

THE HAND I WAS DEALT- FREE WEB SERIES

NOW AVAILABLE ON YOUTUBE!

YOUTUBE.COM/SILKWHITE212

To order books, please fill out the order form below:

To order films please go to www.good2gofilms.com

Name:_____

Address:_____

City: _____ State: _____ Zip Code: _____

Phone:_____

Email:_____

Method of Payment: Check   VISA   MASTERCARD

Credit Card#:_____

Name as it appears on card: _____

Signature: _____

Item Name	Price	Qty	Amount
48 Hours to Die – Silk White	$14.99		
Business Is Business – Silk White	$14.99		
Business Is Business 2 – Silk White	$14.99		
Flipping Numbers – Ernest Morris	$14.99		
Flipping Numbers 2 – Ernest Morris	$14.99		
He Loves Me, He Loves You Not - Mychea	$14.99		
He Loves Me, He Loves You Not 2 - Mychea	$14.99		
He Loves Me, He Loves You Not 3 - Mychea	$14.99		
He Loves Me, He Loves You Not 4 – Mychea	$14.99		
Married To Da Streets – Silk White	$14.99		
My Besties – Asia Hill	$14.99		
My Besties 2 – Asia Hill	$14.99		
My Boyfriend's Wife - Mychea	$14.99		
Never Be The Same – Silk White	$14.99		
Stranded – Silk White	$14.99		
Slumped – Jason Brent	$14.99		
Tears of a Hustler - Silk White	$14.99		
Tears of a Hustler 2 - Silk White	$14.99		
Tears of a Hustler 3 - Silk White	$14.99		
Tears of a Hustler 4- Silk White	$14.99		
Tears of a Hustler 5 – Silk White	$14.99		
Tears of a Hustler 6 – Silk White	$14.99		
The Panty Ripper - Reality Way	$14.99		
The Panty Ripper 3 – Reality Way	$14.99		
The Teflon Queen – Silk White	$14.99		

The Teflon Queen 2 – Silk White	$14.99		
The Teflon Queen 3 – Silk White	$14.99		
The Teflon Queen 4 – Silk White	$14.99		
Time Is Money - Silk White	$14.99		
Young Goonz – Reality Way	$14.99		
Subtotal:			
Tax:			
Shipping (Free) U.S. Media Mail:			
Total:			

Make Checks Payable To:
Good2Go Publishing
7311 W Glass Lane,
Laveen, AZ 85339

CPSIA information can be obtained
at www.ICGtesting.com
Printed in the USA
LVOW04s1746131115

462480LV00006B/299/P